The
Nash
Sisters

The Nash Sisters
Copyright © 2019 by Leatha Marie

Printed in the United States of America

ISBN 978-1-946425-52-2

Book Design by CSinclaire Write-Design
Book Cover Design by Pro_ebookcovers

Cover Art by Noyes Capehart, Red Vine II,
Acrylic on canvas 16" x 20", Private Collection

• WRITE WAY •
PUBLISHING COMPANY
RALEIGH, NORTH CAROLINA
www.writewaypublishingcompany.com

The
Nash
Sisters

A STORY OF FAMILY STICKING TOGETHER WHEN IT COUNTS

Leatha Marie

• WRITE WAY •
PUBLISHING COMPANY
RALEIGH, NORTH CAROLINA

CONTENTS

1946
Ethel – Preface. 1

June 1940
Marie – Conversations While Learning about Death 3

July 1941
Ethel – Marie's Father 18

November 1927
Frank – The Big Announcement. 31

May 1928
Ethel – Plans Change 45

1930
Nash Sisters – The Nash Round-Robin Letters Begin. 56

January 1931
Annie – Disaster at Home 71

March 1932
Dianne – Settling Momma's Estate 89

April 1932
Ethel – Visiting Caroline 98

October 1935
Dianne – Conversations While Waiting. 108

1940
Nash Sisters – The Nash Round-Robin Letters 116

August 1941
Annie – Missing My Family. 128

June 1945
Ethel – Decisions, Decisions 138

1946 – Preface

Ethel

MY NAME IS ETHEL NASH. Actually it is Ethel Nash Fox Martin. Don't judge until you understand. I'm one of four sisters raised by our momma after our papa was killed at the beginning of the great war. Momma taught me and my sisters Dianne, Annie, and Caroline to work hard, help your family, and be generous to others—even when they make you mad. Although we were not perfect, the Nash Sisters were interesting. Best of all we knew how to stick together.

In growing up, I learned some big lessons. One very important one is that conversation is the key that opens the mind and the heart. To learn about each other you need to do a lot of talking and listening. The best conversations seem to happen around perceptions of memories and events we thought we were sure of. Knowing when to talk and when to listen is the tricky part. Even when you are certain about something, you may find you do not have the whole picture. Those times can get some interesting conversations going for sure, maybe even shake you up a bit.

There have been great conversations for generations in my family where happiness, tears, laughter, anger, and confusion were shared. We don't really know what we learned until we are older. In the moment, we may be sure of what is going on, like when my first love was to be my husband forever. Then time moves through and changes things. The most significant together moments with my family have marked either celebrations or misery. With either, we talk and tell the truth as we see it, and we laugh when we can.

I am the sister who kept memories while growing up in the 1920s—the decade of optimism, the 1930s—the decade of depression and the 1940s—the decade of war. What a time it was! We didn't know we were poor or missing out on anything. We just were the Nash family. The stories are real—at least how I remember them or was told about them. They are too important to lose, so I share them.

June 1940

Marie

Conversations While Learning about Death

My daughter Marie was a child when she first learned that being pulled into situations of caring for others can be life-changing. My sister, her aunt Dianne, came home from the hospital to "let God take her to heaven." Marie's cousin, Suzy, was not just a cousin, she was her best friend. Their lives were about to change as we began a new understanding of sisterhood.

I KNEW AUNT DIANNE WAS about to die. She had been sick for a long time. It seemed to be all the grownups talked about these days. My momma, papa, and all the others who got together on Sundays talked about whether Aunt Dianne was having a good day or a bad day.

My cousin Suzy is my best friend. We live really close and ride the same bus for school every day. Last week on the bus ride home, Suzy told me that her momma's last hospital visit did not make her better, so she wanted to come home to die. I was struck with sadness, but I could not let it out. I had no right to be sad because Suzy was the most pitiful right now. I moved closer to Suzy so we touched, but I did not hug her. I didn't want to risk being teased by the other kids on the bus. We rode the rest of the bus ride in silence.

The school bus let us off and began turning around as Suzy dashed off, her shoes flying, to the back of her house. Even though there was one more stop before my house, I followed Suzy. I joined her sitting on the back porch steps. She was staring at the trees, watching squirrels dart about looking for somewhere to hide the acorns. My eyes followed hers as I wondered what she might be seeing. I hugged her hard. Neither one of us said anything for a few moments.

Then Suzy let her words flow like water coming down a stream on a rainy day. "Mrs. Gregson has been staying with me while Momma has been sick. Nurses have been coming to care for Momma. Somebody is here every day. I want them to go away. I just want Momma to get better. I want it to be like it used to be."

Suzy lowered her head toward her bare feet. After a few minutes she turned her face to me and asked, "What do they do with children that don't have a momma or a papa? What will happen to me?"

I finally let the tears run. I pulled at the pocket of my dress to find the handkerchief Momma always made me carry. I wiped my tears, blew my nose, and handed it to Suzy. She did the same. Staring at the handkerchief, Suzy said, "Cousin snot. I guess it's better than nothing."

That evening I asked Momma about what Suzy told

me. Momma said, "Yes, it is true. Dianne has been sick for a long time and has decided to come home so she could let God take her." I felt a lump in my throat and my eyes got hot. I didn't know you had a choice about where and when you die.

At dinner Papa said we were staying at Aunt Dianne's house this weekend to be with her. I wasn't sure what this would be like. I didn't want to go except to be with Suzy. But Momma said I was to "pay my respects" to her dying sister. She said I was old enough to witness Aunt Dianne going to be with God. "And besides," she said, "your Aunt Dianne was there when you came into this world, and I want you to be there when she leaves this world." Then Momma said, "Anyway, Suzy will need her good friend around."

We all got up from the table and began clearing away our plates. When I stood, I looked down at my feet and wondered what it might be like to fly up to heaven.

I finally looked at Momma and tried not to cry. "Oh, Momma, I am sorry you are losing your sister. It must hurt an awful lot."

Momma took a moment as if to be careful about her words. Then she bent down and put her hands on my shoulders and said, "Yes, it hurts, dear girl. But Dianne has been in terrible pain for some time. Once she passes on, she will no longer hurt. And that is better than just staying around to keep me company."

I hugged her hard and listened to her breathe. I love hearing my momma's breath. It is so calming and makes me feel safe. Her breathing now was just like always. Slow and steady with her chest moving only a little.

When she stepped away from our hug, I noticed there were tears on her face. She wiped them quickly and went to finish clearing the dishes from the table.

That night I asked Papa to put me to bed. I wanted to talk some more about this but not make Momma cry. He said, "I'll be glad to, little girl, if we don't read that silly book about a woman flying around by an umbrella."

"Papa, that is Mary Poppins! And I love that book!" I exclaimed.

"I know you do, but we've read it over and over. And you always cry at the end. We don't need any more crying tonight," Papa said with that voice that means *and that's all we are going to say about that.*

When it was bed time, I put on my warmest pajamas. Even though it was spring and warm in the house, I couldn't get my body warm. I jumped in the bed and brought the covers high on my neck.

Papa came in and sat next to me on the bed. "So what book are we going to read tonight, little girl? Besides Mary Poppins . . ."

"Papa, I don't want to read. I want to talk about what it means to go be with God."

Then my questions came pouring out. "Momma said Aunt Dianne will go be with God this weekend while we are there. Will I see it happen? Does it hurt? Can I say goodbye to Aunt Dianne? Will she cry? Aunt Dianne, I mean. And what about Suzy?"

Papa and I talked for what seemed like hours. He answered every question and gave me time to ask more. As I was getting sleepy, he said, "Little girl, the important thing for you to do this weekend is remember everything you see and hear. This is an extraordinary thing that you will witness. Death is a part of living, and I think Dianne will do it in a way that will make all of us feel better."

We went to Aunt Dianne and Suzy's house very early the next morning. Momma explained that people from Dianne's church were taking turns caring for Aunt Dianne. This week it was Mrs. Sanders. When we got there, she let Mrs. Sanders go home to rest, and Momma took charge. Momma closed the bedroom door and told people to stay out until she could get Aunt Dianne ready for company. I guess she was bathing her, washing her hair, and putting her in fresh clothes. Momma called Papa in the room, closed the door again, and then we heard furniture moving around.

Not long after that Momma called us in the room, and with a big smile she said, "Now, Suzy, doesn't your momma look fresh as a daisy?" Momma used to say that to Papa and me every time we got a bath, washed our hair, and put on clean clothes.

Papa said that we all had duties to help Aunt Dianne. He put one hand on my head and the other on Suzy's shoulder and said, "She will need help from all of us over the next few days. Girls, we have duties for you."

Suzy and I were in charge of reading to Aunt Dianne, folding paper cranes for her room, and getting ice chips. We had to chop up the block of ice small enough she would not choke on the chips. We kept a bowl of ice ready for anytime Aunt Dianne let us know she was thirsty. Suzy would give her momma some ice with a spoon, and I was the one to wipe up any mess we made.

Aunt Dianne's bed had been turned so she could see outside. After all that commotion, Aunt Dianne was awake and staring out the window. She was smiling—with her eyes. She watched the birds at the feeder, looked at the brilliant color of her flowers in full bloom, and felt a breeze blowing in from the open window. I began to look at those things as she might be seeing them. It was all more beautiful than I had noticed before.

My momma is a good seamstress. She makes clothes and mends things for lots of people. From a paper bag, she pulled out a handmade pillow with a yellow cover she had been working on. On the front of the pillow, in a cross-stitch pattern, was the word SISTER. As she placed the pillow under Aunt Dianne's legs, Momma said, "This will make it more comfortable for Dianne to sleep. A little rise in the legs makes the back lay straighter." I knew Momma had been careful to find the fabric and the filling so it would be just the right softness for her sister.

Suzy and I were good at folding paper cranes. We learned that in Bible School last summer. Suzy's momma let us practice them all the time with different colors of paper. Once we had a few dozen folded, Aunt Dianne would send them to the women at the Whitman's Chocolate Company to put in the tins they sent to soldiers. The paper cranes were also called peace cranes and were supposed to make the soldiers feel better about being in a war.

Papa said, "Aunt Dianne has been fighting her sickness for a while. These cranes will help her feel more at peace."

Suzy smiled and I could tell she liked that idea.

I decided this time we would write something on each one that was a memory of the fun times with her momma. We gathered the paper and pencils, went to the kitchen table, and began folding. After the first few were folded, Suzy just sat there. It was hard for her to get started. "I can't think of anything happy. It's all sad," she said.

So I started. "Do you remember that time we helped feed the pigs with your momma, and you slipped and fell in the pen? She laughed real hard and told us that everyone has to fall in a pig pen at least once. She said to you, 'Now you've done your turn.' Then we all laughed some more, and I plopped myself down beside you in the mud. I am gonna write on this one *1st Pig Pen Fall.*"

Suzy managed a giggle and started writing *Twinkies for Pigs*. When I read what she wrote, I laughed. "That was so fun!" Our memories flashed back to the day that Aunt Dianne brought home a truckload of Twinkies for the pigs.

"Hey, girls, I have a treat for the pigs, but I need your help," Aunt Dianne said as she pulled into our yard. Suzy jumped on the back bumper of the truck and peered over the tailgate. She saw thousands of Twinkies, still in their individual wrappers.

"For the pigs? Why not for us?" Suzy asked in anticipation.

"Where did you get so many Twinkies?" I asked excitedly after I hopped up beside Suzy.

Aunt Dianne explained, "I went to the bake shop and market in town where they sell these. The owners say they can't sell them after they get old, so I can have as many as I want. The pigs don't care if the Twinkies are old. They can eat anything—except the wrappers. Climb inside and take off the wrappers. We are going to give Twinkies to the pigs!"

Suzy and I climbed up and began ripping open the sweet treats, throwing the wrappers off the side of the truck. We got faster and faster at it. After it was too late, Aunt Dianne said, "Don't eat too many, the sugar will go to your head!" We began jumping all over the truck. We landed on top of the Twinkies and laughed like hyenas.

Remembering that day, Suzy and I began laughing all over again. "I think I ate about a hundred of those Twinkies," said Suzy.

"I know, and then you threw them up all over the yard," I teased. It was good to see Suzy happy. If only for a few moments.

Late that afternoon when things were quiet and visitors had slowed, I went into Aunt Dianne's bedroom. I wanted to go in by myself and try to do what Papa said—to remember everything. Aunt Dianne was sleeping soundly. The bedroom was filled with family pictures, treasures, and many things I had seen a hundred times but never really studied. They all seem to be important to her, otherwise she would not have taken such care to place them just so.

Her jewelry was hanging on the wall. Momma said Uncle Joe built her that necklace hanger. It was a wooden frame with three rows of pegs on small boards placed in the middle of the frame. This was where she put her jewelry after coming back from church or an evening out when she dressed fancy. I could see her raise the necklace from her neck, pull it around her head, and carefully hang it on the necklace hanger like she had done time and time again. This was one of the hundreds of things Uncle Joe built for her before he died. He built things for her just because she said she would like it.

The dresser and bureau were covered in flowers, plants, a precious stone, a cross, and other things people had given her. I think all those things were a way of saying how much they love her. She helped so many people. And now they must have been saying thank you.

On the low table by her bed, there was a miniature garden. I know my momma made that with Aunt Dianne. They spent the afternoon in the backyard last fall, searching for the right kind of moss, sticks, rocks, and acorns to add to the planter. When I asked them what they were making, Momma said it was "a land for a person to live in peace." They both laughed out loud.

I don't remember seeing it finished until now. There was a small Asian fisherman carved out of green shiny stone. He was holding a fishing pole with the line hanging in the water. The water was made of something that looked like clear nail polish, and you could see a fish under the water just watching the man with the pole. That fish was not going to go near the line and that seemed okay with the fisherman. There was a squirrel, some geese, and other animals in the planter—none larger than my baby finger. There was a miniature tree just behind the man. Momma called it a bonsai. The quiet fisherman sat looking over his land. He looked like he was at peace. I knew he was watching over Aunt Dianne too.

There were pictures of Uncle Joe in several places around the room. One was a picture of a young Uncle

Joe and another man wearing dark suits. They didn't look very happy but stood tall for the picture. *I'm gonna have to ask Momma about that one*, I thought.

Another was a picture of Aunt Dianne and Uncle Joe during wartime. Uncle Joe had on his private-in-the-army uniform, and he had his arm around Aunt Dianne. She looked lovely in a dark dress with white trim around the collar. Her dark hair was combed and set pretty. They were both smiling so big. Momma once told me that picture was taken on their wedding day.

She said, "I was there when they got married. The day after the picture was taken Uncle Joe went to the war. It was a happy sad day. Happy because my sister just married her best friend and sad because he was going away."

My favorite picture of Uncle Joe is as a young man. He was wearing a work shirt carefully tucked into his jeans. It looked like he had been working in the garden because his clothes were covered in dirt. Uncle Joe was walking down a dirt path toward the person taking the picture. He had a shy smile with his head tipped slightly to one side. He was a handsome man. I know why Aunt Dianne and Momma loved him so. Momma used to say, "Joe is as good a man as anyone could find, just like your papa."

I went to find Suzy. She was in the front room looking at all the Get Well cards that had come to Aunt Dianne. There were so many cards in all the rooms of the house. Suzy had tears on her face. I grabbed her hand in both of my hands and just held on.

Papa said Aunt Dianne was a good person, and we weren't the only people that loved her. I could tell that was true by the cards. Suzy and I walked around the house and looked at all of them. We counted them in groups of ones with flowers, ones with shimmer, and those that were just plain. But they all were pretty and said such sweet things.

"All these cards did nothing. My momma is not going to get well," Suzy whispered as more tears spilled down her face.

Throughout the day, Aunt Dianne lay in her bed. She was sleeping mostly but waking enough to notice the people visiting and talking to her. She smiled with her eyes because I think it took too much effort to do it with her mouth and face. But we knew she was smiling. She would bow her head a little to thank us—for coming to visit, for getting a cup of ice chips for her, or anything else people did for her.

We all knew she was the one that deserved the thanks. Aunt Dianne was Momma's older sister and had given us so much. We lived with her and Uncle Joe when Papa lost his job and we didn't have a house. Even when we moved to our own house, Aunt Dianne would come with her arms full of vegetables and bread. I think she was afraid we might starve.

It turns out my papa is a good cook. I never knew that. Unless Momma was sick, she did all the cooking and cleaning up. She said, "Your papa works hard every day. When he comes home, he rests and I cook. That is just the way we worked things out."

The first night we were at Aunt Dianne's, Papa announced, "Tonight it will be a meal of tradition—turkey, gravy, dressing, green beans, and carrots. A 'thanks giving' meal!" Later Momma told us that the reason he cooked turkey was because it fell out of the freezer on his feet one too many times.

Many people had visited during the day, but tonight was quiet. It was just the four of us at the table for dinner. As I looked around the table, I thought about my momma and papa helping Aunt Dianne go to heaven.

Watching them made me feel happy sad. Happy that Aunt Dianne was getting such love and help for the pain and sad for Suzy losing her momma. Because no matter how good it might be for your momma to pass on, it has got to be horrible for a child. We talked of many things except what was happening. It was like the fact that Aunt Dianne was dying was in every corner of the room and the house, but we didn't want to notice.

Not many people in the house slept that night. Suzy and I were sharing a bed, and we could not fall asleep. We decided to talk about all the kids at school to keep our mind off the sad subject. We went down the list of who sat at each desk and what they were like—who their family was, whether they were nice or smart or just plain mean. We fell asleep as the early morning sunlight was coming in the room.

Later, Suzy woke with a jolt and ran to her momma's bedroom. I was close behind. My momma greeted us at the door of Aunt Dianne's room, "Well, good morning, girls! It is a good morning! Suzy, your momma is ready for her morning hug and reading from your favorite book."

"I think I will read from her favorite book, if that is okay. Momma, would you like me to read to you from the Bible?" Suzy asked.

Aunt Dianne's blue eyes seem to become a brighter

blue. The lines at the sides squeezed upward. Even the lines at her mouth turned up. There was that smile. She had a real pretty smile. I went to get some ice chips, just in case, and Suzy began to read. I saw tears coming from my momma's eyes, but as I heard Suzy reading her momma's favorite book, I couldn't help but feel a little happy.

On Sunday, more people came to see Aunt Dianne and bring food for all of us to eat. They brought flowers from their gardens too. Suzy and I stayed outside most of the day because, as Suzy said, "People are all crying."

Later in the day when the crowds left, Papa called Suzy and me into Aunt Dianne's bedroom. Mama was standing by the bed holding Aunt Dianne's hand. Aunt Dianne was sleeping. I could hear her breathing. It was louder than Momma's breathing. Rather than the almost silent sound that breath usually makes, I could hear rattling like paper being crumpled then opened out smooth and crumpled again.

My papa bent down close to Suzy, put one hand on the bed and lightly patted the space beside Suzy's momma. With a slight smile, Papa said, "Suzy, come sit on your momma's bed." After Suzy crawled up, she grabbed her momma's soft, wrinkly hand.

My papa continued, "Your momma is a good and smart woman, Suzy. She knew this was coming. She made all the arrangements so nobody needed to worry. She told us to tell you about the arrangements when she neared the end. I think that time is now."

He put a box on the bed beside the two of them. Suzy and I had seen that box before. The words

HAV-A-TAMPA were on the outside and inside the lid there was a picture of a pretty lady in a blue dress. We often went to the box to admire that lady with the dark brown hair. One time her momma caught us looking in it. Aunt Dianne scolded us. She said, "You girls stay out of that. It has important papers inside."

Papa opened the box and said, "Suzy, in this box are papers with signatures for all the arrangements your momma has made. We can go through them together later, but we want to tell you about one of the papers now."

He handed her an envelope. Suzy opened it to find an official lawyer-type paper. She just stared at it, confused. Then asked, "What does it mean, Uncle George?"

Papa placed his large hand on Suzy's shoulder and said, "This letter says when your momma has gone to be with God, you will come live with us. We could use your goodness in our house, Suzy, and Marie could use her best friend around all the time. What do you think?"

Suzy turned to her mother who was asleep. She flung herself down by her momma and put her arms around her and cried out, "Oh, Momma, thank you. I am scared to be without you. But I know God needs you. Maybe now I can bear it. You thought of everything. I love you so much!"

My momma quietly ushered Papa and me from the room. Her arm was hugging him close as they walked. She whispered to him, "You are the best husband anyone could have." Suzy stayed there crying for a long time. When the crying got quiet, I peeked in and saw she had fallen asleep on her momma's chest. There were no more noises in the room except Suzy's even sleeping breath. I stood close to the doorway for a few moments listening and watching this amazing moment.

My heart hurt for Suzy but at the same time there was a spark of gladness. Suzy was coming to live with us! That was the best thing ever. I always wanted a sister or brother. Suzy knew me better than anyone and still liked me. I don't think sisters always do that. This was a very sad happy day.

July 1941

Ethel
Marie's Father

Marie was a teenager when I told her about her "real" father. It was the summer I broke my foot. Since I could not walk, I needed her help with the duties of the house and farm. Marie was now my temporary caregiver. A reversal of roles for parent and child. We spent lots of time talking about a life full of happiness and hardship. The days became weeks. It seemed we might run out of things to talk about. I decided it was a good time to tell my daughter about her father. This is a story about what love could and could not be.

FRANK POLLARD WAS MY FIRST beau. He meant the world to me. We grew up together and became best friends. I remember Frank used to tell people that the Pollard and Nash kids were like family. We fuss over each other and make sure nobody messes with us. Frank and I hung out as much as we could the summer of 1927. He was interesting to talk to, treated me like someone who mattered, and he was funny. I like a person that sees things in a funny way instead of being angry about everything. But with all that, our families were different.

The first time he came to church with me was going to be a big day. We planned it all out. We decided it was time to let people know we were serious about being together.

Most of the people walked to church or rode in a buggy back then. Not many in Wilson County had a car, but Frank's family had one. Since Frank just turned 16, he could drive. Me and Frank had planned it all out. We were going to my family church first, the Methodist Church. Frank's family went to the Baptist Church on Sunday and then Wednesday night. I had suggested we go to Frank's church next month. "Let's see how things go with my family relations first," I told him.

Frank asked his parents if he could drive the car to the Methodist Church. The way Frank told me was that his father cared about the car and his mother cared about appearances. His father said to Frank, "You better take care of my car. Not one scratch on it! And if it comes back dirty, you will have to wash it."

His mother had other worries. "We go to church as a family. You can't miss church on Sunday," she said. According to Frank she was raising her voice.

Frank said he was less then truthful about why he wanted to go to the Methodist Church. He figured his real reason would not set right with his mother. Frank told them that he knew a few families that might be able to help them with the farming and that meeting them at church would give him a chance to talk to them. He said his mother protested and said, "Can't you go after church? Most people stay around to talk after the services."

Frank said he told her that would not work because the farmers usually get right back to their houses. Then to appease her, he said, "We will all be at the Baptist Church on Wednesday night. Nobody will miss me for one service." Frank said his father defended his idea and said, "Let him go, Mother. It could be good for the business."

Evidently Mrs. Pollard was not happy about that. Frank said his momma's face turned red, and she blurted out, "Business! That is all you men think about." Frank said his father gave her a stern look and she conceded. Frank laughed and said his mother's next words were, "Okay, go along. But you dress nice! You are repre- senting the Pollard family over there. I want to make sure they know we care about how we show up."

Frank pulled the car in my front yard the next Sunday. I was standing at the window waiting for him, ready to go. We couldn't be late. I began to calm down when he gave me a big smile. That boy had a pretty smile. Perfect teeth and deep blue eyes that smiled when his mouth did.

When Frank walked up to the front door, my heart beat faster. My palms got sweaty. That happened most times I was around him. I stopped at the hall mirror as I went to the door. I smoothed down my hair, pulled at my dress, and grabbed our lunch basket. I wanted to look good for him and all those people that would be looking at us at church.

As he reached the door and started to knock, I flung it open. He jumped and said, "Dang, E, you scared me!"

His eyes never left me and then he said, "Gee whiz, you look nice."

I had already checked him out as he was walking to the door. "You clean up nice too, Frank," I said. I don't think I had ever seen him dressed up before that day. He had on a brown suit. It had darker brown lapels. He wore a white shirt and shoes shined so much the dust just passed over them. I can see him plain as if it was yesterday . . .

Frank said, "This is my funeral suit. Father bought it for me last winter for grandma's funeral. It's already getting too tight, but I thought it would make an impression at church. Maybe they would think you found a real man."

As we walked to the car I said, "When we are at church, call me Ethel. E is the name just between me and you."

"Sure, Eth – el," he said in a way that *el* dragged out, making me laugh.

He walked over to my side of the car, and I gave him a what-are-you-doing look. "A man is supposed to open the car door for his lady," he said as he bowed.

He took the lunch basket from my hand. I looked over at him, gave him a little scowl, and said, "Okay then, but you know I can open my own door!"

"Yes, ma'am, I know you can. You can open any door you want! But today, let me do it for you." He put the basket in the back seat.

Frank could hardly see over the steering wheel, and it made me snicker. "Be careful driving, little man," I said. "We need to get there in one piece." He sat up straight, started the car, and we rolled out smoothly.

When we arrived at church, my sisters Dianne, Annie, and Caroline were outside waiting. They knew Frank was coming today and that he would bring his father's car. Momma was in the church with everyone else. Dianne walked over to the car. Annie ran toward us like she was running a race. Frank was hardly out of the car before Annie ran up to him and gave him a big hug. "Golly, Frankie, you look pretty!" she said, looking at him with those big-as-the-moon eyes of hers.

"I don't look pretty, I'm just dressed up. This is my Sunday-go-to-meeting suit. Do you like it?" Frank replied.

"Yes, siree," Annie said. "Momma is going to like it too!"

Dianne looked over at me and smiled. Then she admired Frank and said, "You sure do look good, Mr. Pollard!"

Frank grinned, nodded his head, and walked over to open my car door. I let him do it without a word.

I hoped Caroline would also approve, but she rarely had anything nice to say.

"What are you trying to prove? That you are rich and better than us?" Caroline sneered at Frank and me like I had broken her favorite keepsake.

Dianne was the oldest and she acted like she was the mom when we were away from the house. She set Caroline straight by saying, "Caroline, there is nothing to prove. Frank and Ethel are just trying to make a good impression. This is the first time Frank has come to our church." And using words that Momma used on all of us, she added, "If you can't think of anything nice to say, don't say anything at all."

Caroline turned her face to the sky and stomped off to the church.

Frank reached for my hand and Annie grabbed his other one. Then we all walked into the church together. I smiled at the picture of us. I was ready to show him off, no matter what people said.

As always, I walked up to the family pew. Momma slid way down the bench to fit in the four sisters and Frank. She grinned at me like she does when I've made her proud.

I remember the sermon word for word. It was an important day.

Preacher Thomas spoke about sin, as he always did. Every week he would spin sin into a story. Today he talked about how hard work—on the farms, in the fields, or in a business—was one way to fight the temptations of sinful behavior. "A man who stays busy raising food from the earth to feed the community is closer to God. He is using God's land for sustenance and to share," Preacher said. "The man who goes to work in an office, whose work helps others, is also close to God. The woman who supports her man is close to God. This is the way family works. Proverbs 18:22 says, *'He who finds a wife that is good receives favor from the Lord.'* "

I could tell Frank was listening because he pushed his shoulder closer to mine when Preacher Thomas said that.

When Preacher Thomas begins to talk his face is kind but serious. His voice is loving and sweet. I knew Annie believed his words, and she would trust whatever he said. We had talked about religion lots of times. She would say, "Preacher Thomas is preaching the word of God. He knows what he is talking about."

About ten minutes into his sermon, Preacher Thomas began to raise his voice, grip the edges of the pulpit, and lean toward the parishioners. "But do not forget—in the Bible we are also reminded what can happen if a wife is tempted by sin." Preacher Thomas was shouting by now, and I began squirming in my seat. Preacher Thomas went on, "Proverbs 12:4 says a wife of noble character is her husband's crown, but a disgraceful wife is like decay in his bones!"

I leaned to Annie and whispered, "Is he talking to you or me?"

Annie whispered back, "You and me are not married yet. I think it is Mrs. Tyler. And you know how much Mrs. Tyler yells at Mr. Tyler—all the time. And I heard she threw a jar of pickles at him for coming home late one time." Momma gave us the *hush-your-mouth look*.

That day was the nicest day. The crabapple trees were beginning to show their fruit and the leaves in the trees were large, making shade where they could. It was warm. Just the kind of day Frank would like a picnic.

I kept thinking, *Hurry up, Preacher Thomas.* I think I even said it out loud once. I looked at Momma and my sisters to make sure they didn't hear. Annie and Dianne's eyes were pointed at the pulpit, like dogs waiting for you to drop a crumb from the table. Caroline was drawing pictures on the church bulletin. Momma was looking down at her hands folded in her lap, deep in thought. She would have smacked me for saying that out loud, so she must not have heard me. But Frank did and grinned at me like he agreed.

I remember wondering what Frank was taking away from this sermon. We had talked about preachers who told a lot of stories just to scare you. We both agreed that there was no point in having a God that said you were evil all the time. We believed in Jesus who was good to all, no matter what.

People would describe the Pollards as snooty, rich, God-fearing people. Well, the snooty part wasn't true about Frank, and he had to save his pennies just like us. He worked hard on their farm. He read a lot and knew about things I didn't, but he never made me feel stupid.

One time when we were down by the creek on a hot summer day, I asked him how he knew so much. He said, "I read a lot. I know about things in books. You know more than I do about real life."

I'll never forget that. I liked that he thought being different could also mean being equal. He was right. Back then I knew a lot about farming tobacco, managing a house while Momma went to work, and growing a garden.

The other thing Frank liked was school. Frank wanted to learn as much as he could at school. He figured he would learn even more by reading books and watching other people make things with their hands. Frank called school a "path to understanding." I learned a lot in school, but for me it was a path to getting a good job someday.

When the service ended, all the people rose to sing the doxology. This was the song Caroline called the creature song. She knew it by heart. Caroline sang loud and off key.

Praise God, from whom all blessings flow;
Praise him, all creatures here below;
Praise him above, ye heav'nly host;
Praise Father, Son, and Holy Ghost.

Then church was over. I was so excited about being alone with Frank, I could hardly wait. I leaned over to Frank and whispered, "Follow me."

I grabbed his hand and headed out a side door. I didn't want to get in that crowd and take time to speak to the preacher before we could get out of there. I told Frank I was starving and that the lunch basket was full of sandwiches, fruit, sweet tea, and banana puddin'.

Frank picked up the pace, and we ran out back, way up the hill, and stopped under the big oak tree. He said, "You stay here, E, and I will get the basket. I can dart around all the people and be back in a flash." He was tearing off his suit coat as he ran to the car.

I found us a good flat place to spread out the table-cloth. As soon as he was back, he started raiding the basket. I smacked his hand and said, "You gotta wait until I set it all out. This needs to be done right."

"Okay, okay," he said as he spread out the picnic cloth. He lay on his back with his hands behind his head just watching me. I liked it when he watched me, so I took my time getting all the food out. Once I was done, Frank reached over and grabbed my waist. He pulled me next to him and said, "You were the prettiest girl in that church. I am glad you are mine."

I let myself fall over next to him, but kept my back straight and strong. "What do you mean I am yours? I don't belong to you, I belong to myself," I said.

"Dadgummit, E, you know what I mean. I know I'll never own you, but I really like being with you. And you chose to be with me. That is all I meant," he argued.

Looking into his blue eyes, I could tell he was a little hurt. I said, "Yeah, I do choose you. Now let's eat."

For what must have been hours, we ate and talked. We shared stories we hadn't talked about before. I told him I'd been thinking about how hard it must be for my momma to raise four girls by herself. He tilted his head just a bit—the way he does when he is thinking seriously. Then he asked, "E, why did your momma have to do it alone? What happened to your daddy?"

I told Frank all about that day we heard the news. Momma raised us four Nash girls in the house her brothers built. She had three little girls and another one on the way when our father left for the war. Just after Caroline was born, Momma learned our father was not coming back.

It was a hot Indian summer that year. Dianne and I were sitting outside on the porch drawing pictures and trying to stay cool. Caroline was crying up a storm, and I could tell Momma was fit to be tied. There was a girl named Lila that came a few days a week to babysit and do some chores. Lila was in the house helping Momma with the baby. Annie was in the yard playing with sticks and prickly seed balls under the sweet gum tree.

A black Model T car drove up to the house and a man in a uniform got out and started walking to the house. I stood straight up and yelled, "Momma, come here quick. Somebody is here just like came to Mrs. Elliott's house."

It was strangely quiet inside. Caroline was not crying

and no one was moving. As the man got to the screen door and knocked, I was frozen. He called out, "Mrs. Nash, may I come in and speak with you?"

Then I heard Momma's shoes shuffle on the wood floors. She slowly walked to the front of the house. When she was in the hall and could see outside the screen door, she stopped dead. She stared at the car like she really couldn't see it. The veins in her forehead began to poke out, like she wasn't breathing. After a moment, in a screeching voice that I had never heard from her before, she yelled, "NO, you cannot speak with me! Not if you have one of those letters! I won't take it. You can't tell me nothing about my James!"

I could see through the screen door that Lila was holding Momma with one arm and Caroline with the other. It was like she was holding Momma upright and without Lila, Momma would fall over. Lila gently helped Momma move to a chair in the front room, right by the hall. Momma sat down but was rigid. Lila looked toward the man at the door and in her soothing voice said, "Sir, you can come in. Just give us a minute."

I sat down on the porch stairs, not wanting to go in. I could see Momma through the front room window. The man walked slowly into the house. I couldn't hear what he said, but I heard my mother scream and cry at the same time. Tears burst out of her eyes like what comes out of the well when you pump real hard. I had never seen her like that before and haven't since. I could see her shoulders heaving as the man handed her a letter. Lila took the letter and said to him, "Thank you. You can go now. We will read this together."

After the man drove away, Lila said to me, "Ethel,

go get your sister." While all this was going on, Annie had run away from the house.

I ran inside and hugged my momma so hard I thought I might break a rib. Then I took off to get Annie.

By the time Annie and I got in the house, Momma was sitting quietly with the opened letter on the table beside her. She was drinking a cup of coffee. Her eyes were swollen, and her face was blotchy red. Annie started shooting questions too fast for anyone to answer. "What's wrong with Momma? Why is she crying? Did you hurt Momma, Lila?"

With Caroline in her arms, Lila walked over to Annie, put her finger on Annie's lips, and softly said, "Shhhh and we can tell you."

Dianne, Annie, and I sat on the floor beside Momma, and she began to talk. She was calm and breathing normal, like when I hugged her every morning. "You were right, Ethel. That was the same man that visited Mrs. Elliott. He brought us a letter just like he gave her."

Hot tears sprung out of my eyes. "What did the letter say?" I demanded. Momma put her hand on my shoulder.

"It is from the War Department. It says your father fought bravely in battle. He was killed but suffered no pain."

I was so angry I rammed my fist into the wall beside her. My voice was loud and full of anger. "He suffered no pain? The heck with that! We still have no father!" Momma did not even flinch at the almost cuss word. She knew I was right. We all knew everything had changed with Daddy dead.

After I finished telling Frank about that day, I saw

his beautiful blue eyes were filled with tears. I moved closer to him, and he put both arms around me. "Oh, E, that must have been so awful. I am sorry." And he kissed me. And I kissed him back. No more words were spoken. Just holding each other and kissing. We stayed up there on the hill way past dusk, getting closer and closer like we were just one person. Then we took off most of our clothes and did something I never had done before.

I told Marie the best thing about loving Frank was making her.

November 1927

Frank
The Big Announcement

The romance between Frank and me was built on years of friendship. We understood that our friendship, which grew into love, was as natural as an acorn becoming an oak tree. After that day under the tree behind the Methodist Church, everything felt different to Frank and me. We no longer seemed like kids who were friends. To Frank, I think love like this meant he was a grown up, even though he was only 16. He began to think about me as his girl and someday his wife and about him becoming a man. Some of what happened that November day I know because I was there, but some of it was told to me later by Frank.

I CARE SO MUCH FOR E. She is so easy to be with. We talk about everything—what's happening in the world since The War, what we wish for in the future, and she even indulges me when I go on and on about sports. She and I were down by the grove of fruit trees one Saturday in November. The trees were in full fall color. It was like we were sitting in a sea of yellow and orange that day. There was a cool breeze, so we sat close to each other. Mt. Rushmore was on my mind for some reason and I said, "E, I saw in the paper that they are almost finished with Mt. Rushmore. You know that mountain where they carved Presidents' faces. Let's go out there and see it someday. Since we are going to travel the US together, let's put that place on our list. I want to see how they carved faces in the side of a mountain."

I'm always planning for the future. E is the practical one. She said, "Just how are we going to get there, Frank? We don't have a car, and you can't afford one."

Keeping my dream alive, I said, "I hear Ford is producing a Model A that will be affordable to most people. Not just the rich. Someday I will be able to buy a $500 car." E seemed deep in thought. She usually likes to debate my dreams until I stop. But today she didn't.

E looked at me, put her hand under my chin to raise my face to hers and said, "Frank, we have to talk about something important." I could tell she was serious so I just listened.

E said, "I have missed my monthly cycle twice now. I talked to Momma about it. She asked if you and I had been having sex. I told her we were petting a bit. She asked if I had been feeling sick to my stomach. I told her I feel like throwing up most mornings. She seemed certain that meant I was pregnant."

There were tears in E's eyes. And they were not tears of happiness. She looked like she was scared. I asked her how we would know for sure. E said her momma said she could go to the doctor and have the test, but then the whole town would know. She said unless the test would make us do something different, there was no need. She also told E if she didn't have a period this month, it's pretty certain.

I know a lot of things but nothing about this. I didn't know what it meant to do something different. All I knew is I wanted to marry her and have a family, and that's what I told her.

Well, I thought I said something wrong because she started crying real loud, and tears came gushing out. I said, "What? What is it, E? What's making you so mad?"

She grabbed my shoulders and put her arms around me and said, "You are the best person in the entire world! I thought you would want me to get rid of it. We are too young to be parents or even to get married. I want to be your wife someday, but I didn't think it would be now!"

I laughed and said, "Heck, girl, don't you know how much I love you? It won't matter whether we get married now or five years from now. I will be the luckiest man in the entire world to have you be my wife! Now kiss me, you fool!"

We did a lot of kissing that afternoon. And we had sex, and it was as wonderful as ever.

Just when we headed for home, it began to rain. Maybe it was an omen. Then I was the one who got quiet. It dawned on me that we had to tell my parents. That would not be easy. My mother would not be as understanding as E's mother. She worried so much about appearances, and she often said she had plans for my life.

In my mind I began putting the plan together

on how to tell my parents, but things did not go as I hoped.

The next morning my parents and I went to the Baptist Church. My mother loves going to church. She says it's wonderful to hear God's words. I think it's more about being seen. She always dresses in her finest clothes and shoes. She also buys Dad and me clothes for church. We all had to look our best. More than a few times she said, "It makes me happy to show off my family!"

Well, I figured I would take advantage of Mother's good mood after church and tell her and my father my good news. We often went to Sally's Diner after church, and I suggested we do that today. More time showing off her family and being in public would keep Mother from throwing a fit when she heard what I had to say.

As we walked up to the church, I saw on the sign placed next to the church door announcing the sermon topic—"Sins of our Day." That made me a little nervous, but who knows which sin the pastor will pick. According to Pastor Brown, most things in life are sins. After the first hour passed, he began his sermon.

He began, "Today I will speak about a subject that might be difficult for the young people to hear. So, fathers and mothers, if you are worried about what your child hears, let them go outside and play."

He paused for a few minutes to let the children go outside. The Sunday school teacher led the children down the aisle and out the door. They all seemed excited to leave.

Pastor Brown started in. "We live in the Roaring Twenties. That is what the papers say. I agree. Our country is roaring with sin. Women wear immodest clothes that show much of their body. Men drink alcohol until they pass out in the streets. Mobsters kill each other just for territory. Families spend money just because they have it. Yes, these are roaring times. Times of sin."

I closed my eyes and blocked out what I was hearing. I didn't want to hear his version of what God condemns or what He looks upon favorably. I knew he would find quotes from the Bible to back up his words. E and I often talked about the Bible being used for whatever people want to believe. There are passages for whatever goodness or sins you want to say is the truth. This made me furious, so I blocked out most of what Pastor Brown was saying.

Then I heard him talk about sex, and it jolted me back to attention.

"People talk about intimate relations in public as if we all want to hear about it. The movies, the music, the liberated woman all indicate that sexual immorality is everywhere. Push away temptation. Use your will to avoid these immoral behaviors. Paul reminds us of God's words in 1 Corinthians 7:2, "*but because of the temptation to sexual immorality, each man should have his own wife and each woman her own husband.*" And in 1 Corinthians: 8-9, "*To the unmarried and the widows I say that it is good for them to remain single, as I am. But if they cannot exercise self-control, they should marry. For it is better to marry than to burn with passion.*"

I looked over at my mother and father. They were listening intently, as they usually do. I was glad they were paying attention. This would be my argument for marrying Ethel.

Pastor Brown went on for what seemed like an eternity, but it gave me time to line up my points for the conversation with my parents. Then I heard the last sentences that the Pastor uses in every sermon. "That is the word of God. Thanks be to God."

As everyone repeated "Thanks be to God," I almost shouted it. My mother gave me a smile bursting with pride at her son loving the word of God. If she only knew why.

On the way to the diner in town, I was putting together my thoughts about the conversation I needed to have with my parents. Mother was eager to know what I was thinking about, and she asked me what I liked most about the sermon.

I was quick to answer. I said, "I finally understand how important marriage is to not being a sinner." Dad raised his eyes to the rearview mirror and gave me questioning look. Mother just looked down at her hands. It is not often that she is quiet when the subject of sin comes up. To me, the silence in the car was curious and funny at the same time.

To fill the silence, I said, "I'll explain when we sit down for lunch." Mother started fidgeting with her gloves, and Dad could barely take his eyes off me in the backseat to drive. I wished I could hear their thoughts.

The diner was packed. I led us back to the far booth. Sitting further from the door would make it easier to have a conversation. I wanted to do this in the diner because I knew my parents would be calmer in public. But I also did not want people to overhear what I was saying.

After our food was served, I placed my napkin in my lap, hooked my fingers together and raised my elbows to the table. Dad usually blessed the meal, but he hesitated. I said, "I would like to say the blessing." They both bowed their heads.

"Thank you, God, for this food and for the enlightenment of Your word." They joined me in the "Amen."

I said, "Mother, Dad, I have been thinking a lot about my life and my goals. Pastor Brown's sermon today gave the timeline for my goals. I want to marry Ethel. If she can be a part of my life as I go away to Blue Ridge School in the fall, I could concentrate on my education. We will get married sooner rather than later."

The first thing out of my dad's mouth was raw and louder than I wanted, "Have you knocked up that girl?"

I could tell that the subject never entered my mother's mind because once Dad spoke, her face moved from a listening smile to wide eyes and her mouth dropped open. Mother sat stiff but moved her eyes to look around us. I could tell she was hoping no one heard her husband. The couple at the counter near us faced forward and dropped their heads toward their plates as if to be invisible.

Then Mother gave herself permission to speak, but only in a whisper. She leaned across the table, her jaw clinched as she spoke, "No, you cannot get married to that girl! She is beneath you. She will always be a farmhand. You need a wife who can support you while you practice law or become a doctor. She does not have the social graces to live that kind of life. And she is a Methodist!" Now her face was flushing red and the veins in her neck were stretched taunt.

I could feel the anger in my voice elevating. But I spoke slowly and was determined to make my point. I said, "Mother, I love Ethel. She is the only one that will love me enough to help me become whatever I decide."

Dad persisted but in a somewhat lower tone, "Answer me, boy. Is Ethel pregnant?"

I summoned the strength to be truthful. "Yes, sir, she is carrying my child. Pastor Brown said today that if we cannot resist temptation of the body, then we should marry. Marriage is the way to bless our love in God's eyes and not be sinners. You both taught me to follow the word of God."

Dad fell back against the booth, threw his napkin in his plate and said, "We are getting out of here!" He grabbed his wallet, tossed some money on the table and got up. "Come on you two. This is no place to talk about this!"

Mother slowly slid across the booth without looking at me. After she followed my father out, I rose from the booth dejected. Having this conversation in the diner had not been a good idea after all.

As soon as we got in the car and closed the doors, the yelling started.

My father's face was practically purple when he shouted, "What the hell were you thinking, boy? You are too young to have a kid; you are still a kid yourself! You know nothing about how hard life is!"

Mother raised her own voice to be heard. "You have ruined your life, Frank! You think getting married will keep you from being a sinner? Well, it is too late for that! Becoming a father before you finish school is foolish! We had a plan. You agreed to that plan! We have provided for you so you could become a successful lawyer. Oh, I don't care; you could be a doctor if you wanted. But you would be somebody!"

I was a bit embarrassed because we were behind glass, not a curtain. People could see and hear us as clear as if we were standing outside the car. Dad must have realized this and threw the gear shift into reverse. We screeched out of the parking lot.

I didn't respond. I just wanted them to get it out. All the way back home they screamed out words and sentences, not always making sense.

Dad was really hollering and throwing out questions. "How do you think you can feed and clothe a child? It takes money! What about a house? Paying for school? A boy of 16 in school can't do any of that!"

Mother managed a lower tone, but it was full of hatred as she tossed her own words at me. "She lured you into this, didn't she? Oh dear God! You don't have to be involved with her baby. It was her choice, so let her be responsible!"

They went on and on. I wished I was seven years old again when Dad would whip me for something I had done wrong and it would be over. I'd rather have that than shouting about it on and on. When we arrived home, I jumped out of the car and ran toward the house. Before I got to the front porch, I turned back to them and shouted, "I will not talk to you about this until you can be civil!" Those were my mother's words coming out of my mouth. I ran up to the porch, shoved open the door, and ran to my room. I slammed the bedroom door and locked it.

I stood in the middle of my room full of loathing for

my parents. I kicked the bedside table as hard as I could across the room. The lamp fell and shattered on the floor. I slammed my fist into the picture of our family that hung on the wall. I began to tear up everything that reminded me I was their kid and not my own man. I threw myself on the bed and yelled every curse word I knew.

During the next several hours Mother or Dad would come to my door and ask to come in or for me to come out. Each time I refused. The sun was setting, and I could smell dinner being prepared. I felt calm again. I began to rehearse the points that would be needed for this debate. It was not necessary for them to agree with what I was doing, just to accept the fact I was doing it. I did not need their permission. If I was old enough to be a father, I was old enough to make my own decisions. I picked up a few sheets of paper that had been slung across the room and began to look for a pencil in the carnage I had created. I started the list of retorts I wanted to make to what they had already said. I am just a kid—my age is not a factor. I am able to do everything Dad can do. Fix things, manage the farm, get a job, and provide for a wife. I wrote a list:

1. *Ethel is beneath me. You don't know Ethel. She is sweet, caring, smart, and knows what she wants. I am glad she wants me. I am the one beneath her in this world.*

2. *She forced me to "knock her up." I have wanted her to be my girl for months and even years. She resisted my advances because she wanted to be sure*

we would not make a mistake. The first time we had sex was proof that we were ready to declare our love for each other. If you want me to describe it to you, I can.

3. *Ethel can't support me as a doctor or lawyer. That is your dream, not mine. I want to be a good man with a farm or a good job. I want to have a family. I will not be in "circles" that would judge who I am. I don't want to be worried all the time, like Mother is, that we are not good enough.*

4. *Money to raise a child. I can make money by getting a job. Ethel is a baker and seamstress. She already is lining up some clients who will pay her. We can both finish school right here in Wilson County—for free. If we can't live here, Ethel's mother said we can live with her until we get on our feet.*

I started a new list with the points I knew my parents would make but had not yet. I needed to think how to respond to those.

> *Who knows about this?*
> *When will we get married?*
> *When will the baby come?*
> *No need to get married.*
> *This affects their reputation in the Wilson County.*
> *Money, money, money . . .*

Mother knocked on the door again and softly said, "Frank, let's talk this out. Dinner is ready. You need to eat. You didn't eat a thing at lunch. Please come to the table."

I told her I would be there in a minute. I heard her exhale like she had overcome a really big problem.

We did not talk about **The Problem** until dinner was finished. Mother rambled on about the weather turning cool, the fall vegetables that needed to be planted, and so on and so on. Neither Dad nor I paid attention.

As Mother cleared the dishes from the table, I said to them, "Please let me talk and you just listen. Let's not shout." There was no emotion in my voice, just calmness because I had thought this through.

"Dad, I know you are upset because you don't think I am old enough to take on this kind of responsibility. Well, I think I am. And I am taking this on. You will not have to be bothered with what you think is my mistake. I will get a job at the cotton mill. They pay pretty well and are always looking for good help. Ethel is a great baker and seamstress. She already has people that pay her for that. After the baby is older she will go after more clients."

"Mother, I know this is not what you planned for me. It actually is not the timeline I planned out either. But I love Ethel as much as you love Dad. Once you fell in love, could you think about not being with Dad? Even before you got married?" She looked lovingly at Dad and shook her head.

I told them Ethel's mother had said we could live with her family, if we wanted to. She has a big enough house. Ethel's sister, Dianne is moving out when she gets married in a few months. Then there will be an extra room. Ethel's sisters Annie and Caroline can help around the house and with the baby while Ethel and I work. I also said since they worried about our family reputation there was another option. I was thinking Ethel and I could move away before everyone knows about the baby. If we decided to move back to Wilson County someday, we could do it long after people have stopped counting the months between marriage and fatherhood.

The tears flowed from my mother's eyes. Dad sat silently with his hands holding his head as if exhausted. I got up from my chair and hugged them both.

I said, "To both of you I want to say I did not intend to hurt or disappoint you. I knew you would be surprised by our news, but I did not think you would hate me for it. You raised me to be a good person. I thought you would support me and be a little proud of how I am taking responsibility."

Then I walked back to my room and locked the door.

I climbed out of the window and walked the two miles to Ethel's house. She and I planned that I would come by after I told my parents the news. When I reached her house, the sky was black but lit by a full moon. There was Ethel, out in the front yard, sitting in the swing that was made for Caroline. Ethel was swinging slowly. As I got closer, I noticed the breeze she was making as she swung. Her dress was blowing, covering the seat and the ropes below her hands. The light from the house appeared just behind her hair. It looked like she was a flying angel. She was so pretty that I could hardly breathe. Once I came into view, she jumped down from the swing and ran over to me. She grabbed my hand. I wanted to kiss her so bad, but we tried not to do that where people could see.

"How did it go?" she asked.

"It was horrible. They are disappointed in me. They think we are too young. They screamed and hollered for what seemed like hours."

I told her most of the rest of the story. She listened so quietly, it felt like I could talk forever. When I paused, she leaned over to me and said, "Frank, that must have been so awful. I am sorry." Those were the words I spoke to her before we made love the first time.

Ethel's mother called from inside the house, "You okay out there? Frank, how did it go with your parents?"

I fudged a bit with the truth saying, "It was okay, Mrs. Nash. We still have some things to figure out."

Mrs. Nash came to the screen door and said, "Frank, you and Ethel will figure it all out. And in the end, we are going to have a beautiful baby! Praise God!"

Ethel and I agreed with that. We are lucky to have each other. I know we are going to work this out but, man, I am a little stumped about how it will all go.

MAY 1928

Ethel

Plans Change

Best laid plans, they say, can come undone. That was certainly true for me and Frank. We were to get married as soon as we could and become a normal family. The Pollards had a different plan, and they made Frank an offer. The baby had different plans too. Here's the way it all went.

AS TIME FOR THE BIRTH approached, Frank worked hard to help me be ready for the baby. It was decided. Frank would not be around for long after the baby was born. He had agreed to his parent's terms. He figured we could have the best of both worlds in the agreement. The marriage would be postponed until next year. He would stay in Wilson County until Blue Ridge School started in September. In return, his parents would pay for Frank's three years of college prep school, buy him a car, and give him cash to live on. We decided, but did not tell anyone, that I would join him in Virginia with the baby as soon as we could.

Our house has four bedrooms. Momma's room, Caroline and Annie shared a room, Dianne's room and my bedroom. Since Dianne would be moving out soon, her bedroom would be vacant. Momma said I could have Dianne's room for the baby. I wanted the baby with me, so we decided to divide my room into two rooms. That way Caroline and Annie could have their own rooms. We would put up a curtain to divide my side of the room from the baby's part. That way we could really have a baby room. Momma said it is best that the baby can't see the momma all the time, day and night. The baby wouldn't sleep soundly and would just want to be in Momma's arms. Since she was a momma of four girls, I guess she was an expert at these kinds of things.

After a long day in school and finishing daily chores at the farm, Frank came to my house to paint the baby's room. I set the table for dinner so Frank could eat before getting started on the room. Every time I saw Frank lately, my face would flush and tears began pooling in my eyes. It was harder and harder to keep from crying.

Dianne said the emotions were probably due to pregnancy more than our situation. During one of my crying jags last month, Dianne said, "You are strong, Ethel. You always have been the strongest of us girls. You will be fine raising this baby without a man."

I had not told my best friend and sister the plans that Frank and I had in mind. I would not be raising this baby alone.

As Frank entered the house, he removed his cap and moved quickly to the kitchen. "Hey, E, how are you feeling today?" he said as he kissed me on the cheek.

"I'm fine, Frank. Just a little tired. According to Momma's calculations, I have one or two more weeks to go. It will be good to get this part over."

Frank's eyes met mine. He gave me a strong hug. There was no need to say anything more. I knew he was mad, sad, and exasperated about what his parents were doing to get him away from me. I also knew he had no intention of fulfilling their command not to be involved with "Ethel's baby." We had talked about this a hundred times since he told his parents that I was going to have the baby—our baby.

Frank released his arms from me and planted another kiss, this time on my lips. I will never forget his lips. They were soft and sweet like ice cream on a hot summer day.

"Okay then—just a few weeks. Let's finish our baby's room," Frank said as he grabbed the biscuit and ham from his plate and moved into the back room.

I picked up the curtain that I made for the room and followed him. The curtain was made of cotton voile print. Momma helped me pick it out. She was so good at sewing and knew what kind of fabrics looked best as a dress, bedsheet, or curtain. I thought it was so pretty. It had a white background with small swatches of green color and darker green plants placed at random. It looked like a garden to me. When I held it up, it softly fluttered in the air. It would be just what we needed.

Frank painted the baby's part of the room yellow, and he repainted my part of the room white. It was making everything all crisp and clean looking.

Momma joined us after coming in from the yard.

She was carrying a bunch of yellow roses she cut from the fence. There was an empty jar on the dresser where Momma had removed the last bunch of flowers. She kept fresh flowers in the room all the time. She smiled and said, "I really like the color you picked. A soft yellow will remind our baby of sunshine. It won't matter if it is a girl or a boy."

As she arranged the roses in the jar, I thought of the fence line covered in yellow roses. Momma often told the story about Daddy planting those roses when they got settled in this new house. Momma's best friend in the world, Ellen, lived in the house on the other side of the fence. Daddy said since Ellen and Momma would spend so much time yakking over the fence, they should have something pretty to lean on. Momma always ended this story with, "And that is how yellow roses became my favorite flower." When she told that story, I thought yellow roses would always be my favorite flower too.

I was in my part of the bedroom while Frank finished painting the door and trim around the room. I was ironing the baby's clothes that had been given to me by the ladies at the church. I heard Frank whistle like men do when a pretty woman is walking by. I could tell he was pleased with his work, so I came in to inspect. When I saw the finished project, I whistled too.

I looked over at Frank with an adoring smile, "Yes indeed, Mr. Pollard, you did an excellent job! I just need to get the rest of the furniture in, and we are ready!"

Frank turned to me and looked at my swollen belly. "I am glad we have a couple more weeks, because I am working on one more thing. I can bring it by in a few days."

"Wait, Frank, I'm not sure we can fit anything else in this room. What is it?"

As he was gathering his things to leave, he said with a sly smile, "I'm not telling. But it is something you will need."

I protested, "Frank, don't get in trouble doing anything at home for the baby. Your parents will be furious, and they will ship you away sooner. Besides, I think we have everything we need."

I could tell he was tired because he did not argue or explain. He just raised his hand in the air as he walked out of the house.

The next morning I asked Dianne if she would go into town with me. Momma had a list of things she needed, and I needed a few more things for the baby. Since we both liked getting out on a warm, sunny day, Dianne jumped at the chance. Besides, Dianne had a list too, if we had enough household money left over after the shopping for Momma and me. I led our mule Sadie from the barn over to the wagon. She was happy to come with me because she knew I had apples in my pocket. She actually followed my pocket, not me. We got Sadie hooked to the wagon. Dianne climbed up to the seat easily. I was struggling to pull myself up.

"Every day it seems you are getting bigger, Ethel," Dianne said. "It looks like you will pop any moment now! And that would be messy!" I finally hoisted myself onto the bench seat. I shoved Dianne and said, "Stop being mean, my bigger sister!" Sadie groaned a bit when I sat down. Dianne just laughed.

After a mile or so bumping along the dusty road in silence, as if in a way to apologize, Dianne said, "Your room looks nice. It was very clever to divide the room so you could have some privacy. You and Frank have done a great job on it."

"I don't know why I will need privacy from my own child. There will never be a man in that room. Since Frank is leaving me, I will not find another man to tell me how to raise my child," I said with false anger.

Dianne skipped over that last comment and said, "When does Frank leave for school?"

"His parents wanted him to leave last October—as soon as they found out he got me preggo! They did not want him to have any part of my mistake!" I said with real anger, and not toward my sister. "But Frank put his foot down and told them he would move out in his own good time whether he went to the Blue Ridge School or not! For now, that means he will be there for fall term. That is September first. So, I have Frank's help a little while longer.

"Let's change the subject, Dianne. I get so darn mad when I think about it. Say something to make me laugh."

Sadie pulled us toward town. She had been up this hill and around the curve so many times, she knew exactly where to go. Dianne began to sing a song we had made up together. It was to the tune of *Jesus Loves Me.*

> *Boys all love me! This I know,*
> *For they always tell me so.*
> *Pretty ones to them belong;*
> *They are weak, but we are strong.*

Then I joined in for the refrain.

Yes, boys all love me!
Yes, boys all love me!
Yes, boys all love me!
But we don't need them no, no, no!

That worked! We started laughing and couldn't stop. We sang it again and again, laughing at the same time. Sadie turned around and did her whinny then hee-haw noise. She was laughing with us! By the time we got to town, my sides and back hurt from laughing and bouncing.

I told Dianne we better stop, because this baby was jumping all around in my tummy. And the laughing was making me pee. Dianne said, "That baby is singing with us! That proves it! It's a girl!"

As Sadie pulled up to the general store, I realized I was not just peeing. It was a lot more, and it was pooling around my feet in the wagon. "Look, Dianne!" I said.

Dianne gasped and said, "This is what Momma called breaking water. The baby will come soon! We need to get to the doctor!"

"No, I think I can wait. I don't feel the pains yet. The baby won't come until the pains start. You take the list and the money and get the things we need in the store," I instructed. "I can't get up and have everybody see me all wet."

Dianne jumped down, then turned to me and said, "I'll hurry, Ethel. I am so excited! We are going to meet this child today!"

Dianne did hurry, and it was a good thing because before she got back to the wagon I felt a pain. About fifteen minutes later, I felt another one. This one really hurt. When Dianne got to the wagon, she saw a look on my face that must have scared her. She threw the bags into the back of the wagon and jumped up beside me. With her eyes wide and bulging, she said, "Are we going to see Dr. Walker now?"

I said, "Yeah, maybe we should. It will take more time to get home, and then someone will need to come get the doctor if I have trouble." Sadie must have known what was going on. As Dianne commanded "Yee Haw," Sadie began to trot. Sadie never went anywhere fast, but now she was running up the road. We got to Dr. Walker's house in no time. Dianne pulled on the reins and yelled, "Whoa, Sadie!" We almost passed the house before Sadie could stop.

Dianne tied Sadie's reins to the railing and dashed around to my side of the wagon all the while yelling, "Hey, Doc! Hey, Doc, I need help here! Doctor, please come outside! We're going to have a baby!"

I told her to shush. "We don't need the whole town hearing this! I can walk, I'm not an invalid."

But she was right. I needed help getting down from the wagon. A pain shot through my back just as I was stepping down, and I fell to the ground. "Doggone it! With the water and the dirt, I look a mess!"

Dianne helped me get up, and we walked into the doctor's office. His wife, who runs the business and helps the doc as a nurse, came into the front room. She took one look at me and said, "Lord, child, did you drag yourself here?"

"No, Mrs. Walker, Sadie brought us. I just thought I'd sit a minute after getting off the wagon," I said, trying to bring a little humor.

"Let's get you cleaned up and in a gown. You can't have a baby looking like a yard rat!" She meant it to be funny, but it made me mad. I gave a look to Dianne. "Mrs. Walker, we can do this. You don't have to stay," I said.

"Yes, I do," she said. "I need to get things ready."

Once I was washed up and in some clean clothes, Dianne grabbed my arm to get me boosted up on the wooden table covered in sheets. Another pain hit. I screamed bloody murder.

Mrs. Walker flew open the door and yelled, "We need the doctor in here right now!"

Dr. Walker finally came. He said, "Okay, okay. Calm down. Someone as young as Ethel will not have that baby quickly. Someone as young as she goes through a lengthy labor period. Dianne, you will have time to go down and get her momma."

Mrs. Walker said, "I think this baby wants out. Ethel's water already broke through, and her pains are ten minutes apart."

Dianne said she wasn't going to leave me, no matter what. Doc stepped in the next room and called to his son, "Philip, I need you. Take the wagon out front down to the Nash house and get Ethel's mother. Don't do anything to worry Mrs. Nash. Ethel will be fine. Tell her it looks like she might have a grandbaby soon, and she should come along."

Evidently Philip was used to this because I could hear him running out the back door and around to the wagon.

The doctor did his examination and said, "Whoa, baby! Slow down! We aren't quite prepared!" He started rummaging through the cabinet and asked his wife how quickly she could get things ready.

"I am ready," she said.

The next pain was a huge one. Dianne said I screamed like a wild animal. The doctor yelled at me, "Don't push!" My response was, "How the heck do I do that! This dang baby won't stay in!" With the next gigantic pain, I passed out. I don't remember anything else.

Dianne told me later it was a good thing I could not see it. She said, "You must have busted a geyser loose! Blood came out almost as much as the water! And when that baby slid out, the doctor was hardly ready to catch it. I screamed in sympathy and fear for you, Ethel. Then the doctor yelled at me—GET OUT!"

As Dianne tells the story, she figured she should leave the room. The doc didn't need two passed out women on his hands. Just then Momma burst through the door and yelled to the doc, "What in the Sam Hill is going on! Help her, Doc, she's bleeding too much! She is just a baby herself!" Dianne changed her mind and decided to stay in the room so Momma would not hurt the doctor. Later Momma claimed she would never have cursed at a doctor. I knew she did because Dianne said so.

Mrs. Walker evidently tended to the baby. Momma and Doc tended to me. I didn't really care who did what, 'cause I was out like a light at midnight. Momma said she heard a smack to the baby and then a loud baby cry. Momma and Dianne looked over at the baby. Dianne shouted, "Thank God! It's a girl!"

"Listen to that voice," Momma said.

Dianne burst out loud laughing with tears streaming down her face and replied, "She has her mother's singing voice!" That's when I woke up Dianne said—when everyone was laughing.

After everything was cleaned up with me, the doc went to sit in a chair. His head was down so his chin touched his chest. It looked like he was praying hard. "Holy smokes!" he said softly. "That was the fastest one I've ever seen!"

They got clean sheets under me and a pillow for my head. I stayed the night at the doctor's office. He said I lost so much blood, he needed to keep a watch on me. Dianne went to find Frank. Momma stayed with me.

"Have you decided on a name, honey?" Momma asked. "The last time we talked you had three or four you were thinking about."

That sweet baby was in my arms already nuzzling at my breast. I could hear her breathing. It was the sweetest sound I ever heard. I looked at my baby's face and said to Momma, "Momma, she is a child I wanted because it is from me and Frank. Even though the Pollards don't want the baby, Frank and I do. I read somewhere that the name Marie means wished-for-child. So, her name will be Marie Frances Nash."

Momma put her arms around the two of us and said softly into my ear, "That is perfect, Ethel. Just perfect." At that point my breathing, Momma's breathing, and Marie's small breath were all the same rhythm.

Yes, Frank went to Virginia as planned, but it turned out Marie and I didn't.

1930

Nash Sisters
The Nash Round-Robin Letters Begin

The Nash girls lead different lives now that we are grown. Marie and I still live in the family home with Momma, Florence Nash.

Dianne got married and moved with her husband so Joe could take a job with Burlington Mills near Greensboro, North Carolina. They could make a better living at the mill than at farming.

Annie finished school and decided to move to a "big city" as soon as she could. She took the train to Washington, D.C. to look for a job and a rooming house. She found both and moved that same trip.

Caroline moved from place to place. She lived with families who needed help with their children or housekeeping. Even though she was good at her job, she did not stay in one home for long. Sometimes she lived at home. She said she could not be a caged bird. She needed to fly.

We stayed in touch by writing round-robin letters. It all

*started when Dianne and Annie moved away. I desper-
ately missed my sisters and decided news about each
other could be a gift. Like a present that arrives in the
mailbox. The Nash Round-Robin Letters began with me.*

Instructions for the Nash Round-Robin Letters

We talked about this when you were last home, but
in case you don't remember the details, here is what was
decided.

Add a letter to the round-robin letters each time the
envelope comes around. I hope we can have the robin go
'round at least once a month. Don't hold the letters more
than a few days before mailing them. Even if you are busy or
can't think of anything to say, just make comments on what
other letters have said. You can write letters front and
back and no more than two sheets of paper to save on postal
costs. Here is the way the Nash Round-Robin Letters will go.

I'll start it since it was my idea. I write my letter and
mail it to Dianne. Dianne, you write to us about your life in
Burlington and mail my letter and yours to Caroline. Since
we are never sure where Caroline will be living next, she has
asked the postmaster to hold her mail. She promised to save
some money for stamps and go pick up her mail once a week.

Caroline, please write your letter as soon as you can, add
it to letters from Dianne and me then send all of them to
Annie.

Annie, you contribute your letter and send all four back
to me. I know you have a Roaring Twenties life to tell us all
about, but please try to keep to two sheets of paper.

When I get the letter from Annie, we have completed one
round-robin. I take out my letter and start it all over again
with a new letter.

My dear sisters – March 5, 1930

Since we were together a few months ago at Christmas, I am not sure I will have much new news to share. Today is Ash Wednesday, and I just got home from church with Momma. Now is a good time to start this letter.

You know that I still have not gotten married. Now that Frank is out of our life I need to move on. I am courting pretty heavy with Lawrence Martin. I call him Larry. I am not sure I told you how we met. Larry travels around towns selling insurance. He found out from Dr. Walker that I had baby Marie a couple of years ago. He came to the house looking to sell me some life insurance. I don't like salesmen. They always have a scheme to wrestle money from you.

He came up to the front door looking dapper in a suit, tie, hat pitched a little to the right, and leather shoes. I noticed he had a handkerchief sticking out of his suit pocket. He did not look like men I usually saw. I assumed that was because he had money, so I decided to talk to him. He told me about life insurance and why a young mother needed some. He said, "It is kind of like a savings account, Mrs. Nash. Let's say you die before your daughter is old enough to work, she is going to need some money to bury you and make ends meet."

He handed me a paper that told the details and said I could read it later. He said he wanted to come by another day and explain a little more.

Well, he has been coming by "to explain" almost every week for two months now. I enjoy his company. He tells lots of stories about places in the South where he has traveled. Next week he is driving to Atlanta to set up a new office for the company. He will be gone for a few weeks but says he wants to come back soon. I haven't bought any insurance from him yet. That might be why he keeps coming back. I want to think that it is because I am a dashing young woman who is funny as all get out. That might be true, because I clean up good and I tell stories about our crazy mixed up family all the time.

Last week, Mr. Frank Pollard sent me a letter begging my forgiveness, again, for leaving me "helpless." His exact words were, "I know it must be hard to raise a baby on your own. I pray that you will come to your senses and move up to Virginia so I can be a part of Marie's life." Ha Ha. He better pray. If I ever see him again, I will slap that pretty boy face! He left me. I did not leave him. And besides I am the best mother in the world for Marie. We don't need a man!

I know what you are thinking—"Shucks, Ethel, you are only so great at mothering because you have Momma and Caroline around." Well, you are right about that. But I will never let him know I have help.

Speaking of the Pollards, they have moved out of the county and up to Raleigh. Mr. Pollard opened a bank up there, and I hear Mrs. Pollard is entertaining flocks of rich wives. I know she thinks she is the cat's pajamas. There was an announcement of the bank opening in the paper with a picture of them. Mr. Pollard was shaking hands with the mayor of Raleigh and there were other business folks standing around them. I'd send you the article torn from the paper, but then our letter would get too heavy.

That is all for now. I miss you all terribly.

Your loving sister,
Ethel

Hey y'all! It's Dianne here! - March 19, 1930

I am so excited about these letters. I will try to stick to the rules, but I have so much to tell you. I'll try to write small. If this fat letter makes you go over the postal costs, I will pay you all back. I see these letters as a way to keep a diary for years to come, so I am going to tell you some things you may have heard, but I want it in the official Nash Round-Robin Letters record.

Joe got a good job at the Burlington Mills textile plant. His title is bobbin carrier, but that doesn't mean he carries bobbins. He works in the area where the cotton is pulled from the bale, twisted, and spun into thread. Although I haven't seen inside the plant, Joe said the process is the same as our grandma's spinning wheel, only motorized.

His job is to watch all the action really close and fix problems when they happen. He says machines get too much dust if the thread is damp. Then all kinds of problems can happen. He learned how to do this job by being an apprentice with the overseer. To me, it seems nerve-racking to be there ten hours a day making sure nothing goes wrong. And he is walking around all day with barely a break to eat his lunch. He says it is hard work but better than farming! And they give him money to do the job every week.

Joe started his job in September. I stayed behind to pack up our stuff and get the house picked up so y'all would have more room. When I arrived in October, there was a house ready for me and

Joe to move into. It was a perfect house with two bedrooms, electric lights, indoor bathroom with water pumped from the well right into the sink! Isn't that the bee's knees!

Until you come visit and can see for yourself, I'll tell you what the house looks like so you can see it when you read my letters. It is a wooden house painted gray. The trim is white, but there are no shutters. If you are standing in the front yard looking at the front door, you will see a small porch on the right side with an overhang from the roof. It is big enough for one or two chairs, that's it. When you look to the left, you see a room that juts out from the rest of the house—that's our bedroom. Once you come in the front door, you are in the hall. On the right is the "living room" as they call it these days. That is where we sit, talk, and listen to the radio now that we can afford one. It has a fireplace that burns wood. There are four windows in there. I can't wait to sew some curtains.

Behind the living room is a kitchen big enough for a table and four chairs. I love that kitchen. The stove is electric, not wood burning. There are plenty of kitchen cabinets. And guess what? The ice box is electric too! It really isn't an icebox! It is a refrigerator! The indoor bathroom is between the two bedrooms on the left side of the house. I just hope the toilet washes out easy, so the room doesn't smell like an outhouse. And like I already said, the water can pump right into a permanent sink. Can you imagine! I can't wait for each of you to visit. We will have a bedroom waiting for you!

It took me awhile to get the house all set up. And I am not yet finished because we don't have a lot of furniture. But I have done what I can for now. I was thinking I would be bored after that, but it didn't happen. Once I settled us in, the neighbors came calling. The houses on our road are mostly for women and families whose husbands or fathers work in the mill. I really like a few of the women. Some of the others not so much. They want to find out what kind of furniture you have and where your people came from . . . you know, the nosey type. There was one woman that told me to stay away from her husband. She actually said, "The new girls that move in want to be with my Billy. Even though he tries to discourage them, they find their way to his bed." Can you believe that? It is a woman's fault that Billy sleeps around! I wonder how good looking Mr. Irresistible is?!

There evidently is a garden club in this town. I will have to join. I miss using the earth to bring food and beauty. There is nothing planted around this house or on the street. Ethel, next time I come home I will dig up some of the things there to replant here. One thing I want for sure is some of those yellow roses.

Ethel, I am glad you have someone courting you. You and Marie need a man around. If he is as nice as you say, it would be good for her to know a man that won't leave her.

Okay, that is it. My hand is tired and I made it

under two pages. Send it back quickly. Joe says he
will put up a mailbox for my letters this weekend!

Love to all my sisters,
Dianne

Dear Ethel, Dianne, Annie — March 28, 1930

I have had these letters a week. I will take them
back to the postman this afternoon. I don't have much
to say because my life is terrible. There is nothing
new that Ethel does not already know, but she said
I have to write something anyway without any cuss-
words. She told me there is something good in any
day. Well, I will write about me and you can find if
there is any good in it.

The Murphy kids, Michael and Ellen, ages 8 and 6,
are easy to take care of. Mr. Murphy is never home.
He travels all the time. And Mrs. Murphy is having
sex with the doctor's son. You all remember Philip
Walker, right? Dianne, you told me he was the one
who went to get Momma when Ethel had Marie. Well,
it seems getting a person's family to come to the
doctor's office is not the only thing he is quick with.
Last week, I walked the kids home from school. We
came in the back door so we could go right to a snack.
There was Mrs. Murphy without her top and Philip
stripped down to his underdrawers, hugging and
kissing each other right on top of the kitchen table!
In broad daylight! I turned around to Michael and
Ellen and shouted, "Stop! Your momma's busy right

now." But I was not quick enough, because Michael yelled, "EEYOU! Gross!" I grabbed their shoulders and pushed them back out the door.

Mrs. Murphy started shouting and screaming like someone had hurt her. She cussed at Philip and said, "I told you to leave me alone! Now get out of my house, you creep!" I didn't look back, but I could tell Philip was not the only person being a creep.

All three of us walked as quickly as we could. Michael was asking a hundred questions—"What was Philip doing to Momma? Where were their clothes? Are we going to tell Daddy that Philip hurt my momma?" Ellen was just crying and sniffling the whole way. She did not have anything to say about what she saw. I told the kids we were going to my house, and we would eat dinner there. And if they wanted to, they could spend the night, but I was not going to answer any questions about their momma and Philip Walker. I said, "The only thing I will say is that your momma did not get hurt. She should be the one to tell your daddy, not you."

Once we got to our house, I told the kids to go to my room and close the door. I went out behind the barn and started shaking. I was shaking so hard, my body slammed me to the ground. I started screaming and hitting the dirt with my fists. I stayed out there until Ethel called out to me. Then I started breathing deep trying to calm myself down. After a while my breathing slowed, and I started crying. Ethel found me. She sat down beside me and hugged me for a long time. She said in that sweet-momma-kind-of-voice, "It will be okay, Caroline. Whatever it is, it will be okay." Ethel is good like that.

Before we finished dinner, someone knocked on the door. I had not had a chance to tell Ethel what we saw. Michael and Ellen were right under my feet the whole time. When I heard the knock, I stiffened and said to Ethel, "Take the kids to my room, and I will see who is at the door." She must have seen my fury because she did what I asked without any questions.

As I was walking to the door, I was planning what I would say to Mrs. Murphy, but it was Philip Walker at the door.

Now that I could see him with his clothes on, I noticed him different. Philip is a few years older than me. He is a head taller, and he looked like he had muscles. I thought to myself, I don't think I can take him, so don't push it with him.

He said through the screen door, "Caroline, can I talk to you? Outside?"

I said, "No, you cannot! I am not gonna to be alone with you. If you have anything to say, say it right here!"

He said, "Okay. You saw what happened. She is going to the sheriff to say that I attacked her. You know that was not what happened, right?"

I told him I didn't know anything and that I wasn't gonna help him with nobody!"

He told me he could hurt me if I didn't speak up for him. He said, "She went after me just like she always does."

I slammed the door in his face and locked it. Then I started shaking again.

I quit that job and am living with another family in a nearby town. I am not keeping children. I'm cleaning house. I know you all are laughing at that because I am not good at cleaning. But I am a heck of a lot better at cleaning than this family.

That's all I'll say for now.

Caroline

My dear Nash sisters – April 4, 1930

Oh my God, Caroline, how terrible! I can't find anything good in that story except you got out of town! Dianne, how wonderful for you in Burlington! It sounds like Joe is working hard. Ethel, I am glad you are enjoying the company of a good man...I think. How is Marie, Ethel? You didn't say much about her.

As you can see, I am typing my letter. We use typewriters all the time in the secretarial pool at work. I am staying after work to type this letter. Maybe I can write more on two pages than when writing by hand.

I knew I would love getting letters from all of you at once, but this is hard. I want to be with you all right now. And at the time you were going through the things you describe. I want to hug you all. I can't wait until we will be home together again.

My job at the bank is interesting. They set me up in a typing class. I work on the third-floor writing correspondence for the directors of the bank. There are three of us doing this work, and we get along well. The other girls are about my age, and we often go out after work where we could find a place to drink champagne and listen to music. It is not as easy to find in Washington. Not like you can find bootleg liquor in NC. But we were clever and found a few "blind pigs" (that is what they call them here). I never have to pay because one of the women has a company account she can use at all the places we enjoy. That's just the cat's meow! Fun and free!

I am learning some new dances. At just about every club, there are men looking for women to dance with. Sometimes the club owner teaches couples to dance. The Charleston is my favorite. It is really easy to learn. They say it is the rage in the Big Apple. Last week we learned the Foxtrot. That is a dance where you have to really watch the man's movement or you will step all over his feet. I got the hang of it after two nights going out to the dance halls. I can't wait to teach you when I get home. We can buy a phonograph and some records. Even Momma will love it.

Dancing does not require a relation-ship. Just someone to dance with. At the boarding house, the girls that live here dance together as partners in the parlor on Wednesday night. So fun!

I am working for men, dancing with men, and going out with men occasionally but have not found any #1. I am not in a hurry because I love being my own woman. I do what I want, go where I want, and will not get hurt by a man. I also am able to spend my money anyway I want.

I marched in a rally two weekends ago. We went all the way from the White House on Pennsylvania Avenue to the Capitol. Did you realize that even though women were given (given?) the right to vote in 1920, most women do not vote? The men who are elected to represent us do not think about how women and families will be affected by their newest law. Since Jeanette Rankin from Montana, the first woman in Congress, is no longer in the House of Representatives, there is only one woman representing our voice in the Congress, Senator Rebecca Felton of Georgia. There are mostly men deciding to go to war, allow child labor, and other mandates that would be different if women used their voices. The rallies can make a difference! It gets our view in the papers and on the radio. I know the Nash sisters have always voted. Now we need to vote women into public office!

Hey, Caroline, do you think Mrs. Murphy

would run for office? It seems like she knows how to get what she wants from a man! Or at least get what she needs from a man! Ha Ha!

One last piece of news. I meet so many interesting people in D.C. I want to tell you about Jane Hines. We related to each other on growing up in the South. Jane is from Virginia and grew up the way we did -- farming, poor, and with lots of siblings. She told me about getting her degree in psychiatric nursing from the Medical College of Virginia. She was visiting D.C. to talk to people in Congress about what she called "problems of the mind." I was fascinated with how they are thinking about mind illnesses people have.

Remember Uncle Elmer, Momma's brother? They used to say he was a mean son of a gun and drank too much. Jane was educating me about new techniques to improve the care for people like Uncle Elmer. You know they threw him in jail for months and would not let him come home. According to Jane, they have found better ways to help people like Uncle Elmer. If we had known this back then, they probably would have said he was mentally ill, not just mean and a drunk. Jane works in Raleigh at Dorothea Dix State Insane Hospital where they are studying better ways to help those with mental illness. This in little old Raleigh, North Carolina! How about that! Jane said at Dix they are investigating different therapies and remedies. And she said it is working. I want us to go visit her sometime when we are all home. I think you would like Jane. Until now, I have never been interested in college. The secretarial courses I took were all I needed to keep a good job. I thought that would be the end of my school days. But maybe not.

I can't wait for the next letters! Sorry I went on a little long on this letter!

Love you bunches,
Annie

January 1931

Annie
Disaster at Home

Our momma died just after Christmas 1930, leaving Dianne, Annie, and me to work out the details of the estate and Caroline's care.

The Nash girls have not been together since Christmas 1929. Our lives were all so different now that all of us lived away from each other. It was good staying in touch by writing the Nash Round-Robin letters. Since Caroline was included in those letters, not much was shared in them about her fits of anger and sadness. Momma and I had been making decisions about what needed to be done. Annie was especially anxious to get home to see Caroline. Since those two were the youngest, they held a special friendship.

Here Annie tells about her Roaring Twenties lifestyle and a shocking visit home.

I have a car. Actually, I have two cars. But the larger one would be better for this trip. Rather than take the train from Washington, D.C., to go home as I usually did for the holidays, I drove the 1927 Nash. I could imagine my sisters' excitement when they saw a Nash sister had a Nash car! There will be many things to settle with Momma's estate, and the larger car will come in handy for all of us. Besides, I want to show it off to those busybodies that lived nearby. They needed to know that this Nash girl is doing just fine.

I pulled in the driveway at the home we lived in all of our young lives. Even though it looks different now, each time I come home, I visualize it the way I wish it would always be. Four little girls with a mom that made us feel any dream could come true. As I looked at the house, there we were again as children. Dianne and Ethel up on the front porch setting up house with their dolls. Me pushing Caroline in the swing in the front yard. I pushed her so hard her feet almost touch the sky. Those were such happy times.

It had taken six hours to come from Washington with a stop for a sandwich and coffee. Less time than I thought. I surprised Ethel and Dianne by bounding up to the house, throwing open the front door, and shouting, "Tootles! I am here!" as if nothing would begin until I was home. My sisters jumped to their feet and sprinted over. We all grabbed each other in a three-woman Nash hug.

"Well, look at you," Dianne said. "That is one great looking fur coat!"

"How was the drive? Was it cold in that drafty old car?" Ethel asked, reminding us that in one of the Nash Round-Robin Letters I complained about the Model T "horseless carriage" that I had been driving to work.

I filled them in on the new car and said it was not cold at all. The heating system worked great in my 1927 *Nash* Ambassador! Of course, they both wanted to see it.

From the front porch they could see my green marvel. "Holy Moly, Annie!" Ethel said in disbelief. "How can you afford that thing?"

"Antonio, my new boyfriend, wanted to buy me a car, and I told him this one would do just fine."

"Antonio? Not Jimmy you told us about in the last letter? Or that one you were seeing last Christmas? Oh, what was his name?" asked Ethel.

Dianne said, "His name was Woodrow. The pictures of him were hilarious with his wiry yellow hair and long nose."

I chuckled and said, "Yeah, Woodrow. He reminded me of Sadie. Nope, Antonio is my newest beau. His parents came to D.C. from Italy. His father works for the Italian Embassy. Toni is sooo dreamy!"

I had much more to share about my life, but that could wait. I wanted to know about Caroline. My throat tightened and my eyes filled with tears. As we went back in the house, I said, "How is dear Caroline? I am so sorry she is still not well."

Ethel tried to explain, "Caroline is breakable. I never really knew that before. In my mind she was always like a bull. Whenever she got upset, she would throw a fit, not in a fragile sort of way but in a pig-headed way.

Ethel told a story I had not heard. "One day a year or so ago Caroline and her friend Ellie got into a fight. Actually, Ellie did not fight, but Caroline did. Caroline had snitched on the Smith boy to his dad about skipping school. Ellie told Caroline that she needed to stop being so mean. Ellie said, 'You know his dad is going to beat him senseless. It is not your place to get him in trouble.' The way Ellie told it, Caroline got stiff and her face turned red. It was as if Caroline stopped breathing for a minute. Caroline then moved back from Ellie and burst out screaming and spitting curse words at her. Ellie just stood there staring at Caroline wondering who Caroline had turned into. Then Caroline picked up a rock and flung it at Ellie, hitting her just above her right eye. When the blood gushed out everywhere, Caroline ran away."

Thinking about the situation with Ellie, I began to look back on the times Caroline could not control herself. She is a lot sicker than any of us thought. I was beginning to understand that Caroline being in Raleigh at Dix Hill hospital really was the safest place for her to be.

To comfort each other we did another Nash girls hug, but longer and softer this time. Dianne reminded us of our work together. "Okay, we can't be crying about Caroline the whole time. We have work to do to take care of things for Momma. Annie, go get settled in your room. We will have supper ready very soon."

After arranging my things in my old room, the one I used to share with Caroline, I walked to Ethel's room to see Marie. She was fast asleep in Ethel's bed. I could tell by the rumpled covers that Ethel had snuggled next to Marie. Marie was still the prettiest child I had ever seen. At age three, she had changed a lot. Looking less like a baby. She still had that jet black hair like Ethel, deep blue eyes like Frank, and the smoothest porcelain skin. My body felt like jelly standing there watching her sleep. I was filled with love and a pinch of jealousy.

I ached for a baby—to be a momma.

I came downstairs to the kitchen where Ethel was cooking Momma's chicken pastry. It smelled wonderful. I was still sad and a bit depressed about what we needed to do. "How are you two? Were you both here when Momma passed? I am glad you sent that telegram to come quickly. I wish I could have come sooner. Have you decided about the funeral and burial?"

"I was here," Ethel said. "She passed in her sleep as peaceful as a butterfly resting on the window sill."

Dianne pitched in, "Ethel sent me a telegram too. I was able to come right away. The only thing we have decided is that Momma will have her final resting place on the hill on the east side of the property. The morning sun will make her happy. And besides, remember that is where we buried Daddy's few possessions from the War Department."

The memory of dealing with my father's death was faint. I was only three or four at the time. But that resting place was very important to this land. I said, "Of course."

As we ate, we talked quietly about how our family had gone from six to five to four and one of the four of us was . . . not well enough to be home. We were not the same family that played, got into mischief, and kept secrets together. Even when I was very young, I understood how great it was to have sisters who shared advice about life with me. I was never afraid of what might come because they were there for me. Now it felt more like standing on a small island in the middle of a vast ocean rather than the ten acres of home that always kept me safe.

After we finished dinner, I cleared the table. Dianne, the organizer, said "I have made a list of what we need to talk about. Momma didn't leave a Will nor any notes about what she wanted done with her things. We never talked about what should happen to the house and the farm. The urgent piece is the funeral service. Now that you are here, Annie, we can make some decisions."

There was that ten acres of love and loyalty again, holding me steady.

Ethel went to the cabinet high above the stove and pulled out a bottle of wine. I was astonished. I didn't know they drank. But I was also relieved because I needed a drink right about then.

We talked all evening, rarely sticking to the list but getting back to it eventually. Dianne divided up duties. Ethel would talk to a lawyer about what needed to be done with the estate. She knew someone she trusted. Mr. Wilkins helped her deal with the mess of keeping Frank and the Pollards away from Marie. Dianne would make sure all the bills had been paid and find out exactly how much money was left. And I, since I was the creative one, was to plan the funeral and burial. UGH!

"What about Caroline?" I asked.

"There's not much she can do from the mental hospital. But we need to keep her informed," Dianne said.

Then Ethel remembered my closeness to Caroline and said, "Annie, do you think you can write some notes for our discussion about Caroline? I hope what you have learned from your friend Jane will enlighten us."

I agreed to write the notes. The ten acres surrounded by a deep moat and truly inaccessible to

Caroline, my dear sister. My friend Jane was going to help us build a bridge to Caroline.

Ethel, who was closest to the details of Caroline's care, told us Momma had settled with the doctors. "Momma arranged for Caroline to live at Dix Hill through the next year. They say it will be at least that long before Caroline gets better."

When I am anxious, I take charge. I try to control something. I said, "We must go see her right away. I want her to come home at least for the funeral. We are all here. We can take care of her for a few days, can't we?"

Dianne dropped her head as if she was praying and said, "I am not so sure about her coming home. Yes, we can go see her and talk to the doctors. She doesn't know about Momma yet. It will be really hard for her. She has always thought she was Momma's favorite." At that we all smiled. We all thought we were Momma's favorite. That is the kind of mother she was.

The following morning was busy. We were all working to check off our duties on the list prepared by Dianne. It was one long list that required us to document our progress every couple of hours.

I was sitting in my childhood room in the green upholstered chair. Momma had the frame made for my fifteenth birthday. She covered the frame in wool from our sheep and upholstered it in a fabric as dark as a Christmas tree. "A woman needs a proper chair for reading and planning," she had said.

I created a full page of questions I thought we should ask Jane Hines. It was quite a coincidence that I met Jane in Washington, never knowing I would need her expertise with my family. I would talk more about Jane and her work during our car ride to Raleigh. I assumed Jane had met Caroline by this time and would know what therapies might be working. We would meet with Jane at Dorothea Dix first, and then see the doctors before we visited Caroline.

I went to the kitchen where Ethel was preparing lunch for us. Dianne was sitting at the wooden kitchen table Daddy made for Momma when they got married. All the years of moving plates, bowls, and cooking utensils around on that table and sitting together having conversations had made the wood as smooth as silk. Dianne was scrutinizing piles of papers, notes, and envelopes of legal documents.

I walked over to where Marie was playing with cups, a few pots, and spoons. I smiled at her, and she yelled "Annie!" I felt a tug at my heart. To avoid the tears that might come, I sang back to her "Marie, Marie, the wonderful Marie! The best child in this fam-i-ly!" I leaned down to her with my arms out to ask permission to pick her up. Marie raised both arms saying, "Annie, Annie."

I kissed Marie's neck, saying in a sing/song voice, "I am gonna get your sugar. Can I have your sugar?" Marie began a belly laugh which made Ethel and Dianne turn and watch. The laughter of a child is the best sound in the world.

I rocked back and forth holding this precious little Nash girl, the next generation, as I was watching my sisters. Marie and I went over to the table where Dianne was working. I pointed to Dianne, and asked Marie, "Do you know who this is?" Marie leaned forward with her arms out asking to go to Dianne and said "That's Aunt-ee Diann-ee." I cackled!

Dianne tried to act as if she was mad and said, "No, siree, little lady. I am not holding you until you call me Dianne not Auntie Dianne. I am too young to be anybody's auntie." But Marie persisted with the urging of her little arms, and Dianne pulled her close whispering in Marie's ear "Dianne, good Dianne, lovely Dianne."

While I helped Ethel make sandwiches, I reminded them that we needed to get ready to leave because we had a lot to do at Dix Hospital before we would see Caroline.

Ethel said, "I agree. We'll take these turkey sandwiches, apples, and sweet tea with us. We can have a picnic in that fabulous car! Can you eat and drive, Annie?" I told her there's lots of things I could do while driving. Dianne's quick retort was, "I don't want to know!"

I was proud of my new car, so I made sure Ethel and Dianne got the full tour. Ethel was not impressed. Her words were, "I don't know why somebody needs this much luxury!"

"You will after we make this trip. It's worlds away from having Sadie pull us to Raleigh," I told her.

Dianne, always wanting to raise the level of positivity in a conversation, encouraged me to tell about the car. She said she could not wait to ride in it.

I made sure to point out all the features—the French style roof, the four doors, and plenty of room for five or six people. I showed off the mohair velvet upholstery and the walnut wood trim. Oh yeah, and the lever I can move when it is hot that pushes the bottom of the windshield out to let a breeze come in. Such a smart design! The floor is so large that Marie can play all the way to Raleigh. Toni was so sweet to buy this one in green. I love green. When I told them Toni had paid just over $2,000 for it, Ethel's eyes opened wide like a bullfrog and her mouth dropped. She said, "Good God, $2,000! I could buy a lot of land for that! Maybe we shouldn't eat in there! Let's get some towels to make sure we can clean up any spills."

Dianne snickered and asked me what I had to pay Antonio. I rolled my eyes and gave a coy smile. We all giggled. They really did not want to know.

We made a place for Marie to sit in the backseat and a safe place with blankets on the floorboard for her to play with the toys and books we were bringing along. Ethel sat in the back to keep her company. Dianne rode in the passenger seat up front with me. For January it was a nice driving day. The roads were clear of snow and ice because the temperature had been above freezing for several days.

I talked for an hour about what I learned from Jane Hines about Dix Hill and how they care for people there. Each resident rooms with another person, just like they might at home. Of course, some of the very ill are in the hospital section on a ward with others.

Ethel explained that Caroline was in a home with four bedrooms and five other women and said, "There is also a caregiver who lives on campus who is assigned to a group of patients. Everyone in the house must help with cooking and housework. Those who are able are assigned a job in the Dix Hill community. Caroline wanted a job in the nursery taking care of the babies."

That distressed me when I heard about the children. I blurted out, "You mean there are babies in the insane asylum? That is awful. How did they get there?"

Ethel said that they were either born after their mother came to Dix Hill or mother and child entered together. She said there are child carers who keep them safe, clean, and also nurture and love them as any baby deserves. She had seen all this when she went with Momma to take Caroline there the first time. She assured Dianne and me that the space was clean and colorful with lots of things for the children to play with.

Then there was silence in the car as we all pictured what that might be like to be a child there. Ethel pulled Marie into her lap and held on tight. Marie looked into her mother's eyes and said, "Momma, sing the Rock a Bye Baby song."

Ethel began humming a lullaby that our mother had sung to all of us when we were young. All three of us began to sing. I sang through the sadness of wanting my own child.

Rock-a-bye, baby, in the tree top
When the wind blows the cradle will rock.
When the bough breaks the cradle will fall
Down will come baby, cradle and all.
Baby is drowsing, cozy and fair.
Mother sits near in her rocking chair.
Forward and back, the cradle she swings
Though baby sleeps, he hears what she sings.
Rock-a-bye, baby, do not you fear.
Never mind, baby, Mother is near.

Wee little fingers, eyes are shut tight
Now sound asleep – until morning light.

Before the end of the song, Marie slumped down onto the back seat and was fast asleep. The next 30 miles were quiet. Marie slept soundly, lulled by the road noise. We had covered most of the things we needed to discuss earlier in the ride, but we hadn't talked about what Caroline should know about Momma's passing. I broached the subject quietly. I thought we should be honest with Caroline. I knew if it was me and my sisters kept this from me, I would never forgive them. My friend Jane says they tell a patient as much as the patient can handle. It seemed to me Caroline was doing well there. She had a job and everything.

Dianne agreed. She said, "Yes. If we cover this up it will come out at some time in our letters or just future time together. I am worried, though. If we tell her and then leave this afternoon, we might do more harm than good. Remember that Caroline always takes a while to understand things. Her anger or sadness usually doesn't come out when something happens. It comes hours or days after. Maybe we should stay over one night in Raleigh and visit with her again tomorrow."

With Marie fast asleep Ethel knew it was okay to tell me more details about the episode with the Murphy children and Philip Walker. She described how long it took Caroline to get over that. Ethel said Caroline stayed in her room for more than a week. She and Momma took her meals to her there. Although Momma didn't know what happened to Caroline, she wasn't really worried. Momma told Ethel, "Caroline has a tender heart. It gets broken easily, and it takes a while to mend." Ethel said she let it be because she didn't want Momma to know this was something more than a broken heart.

Dianne asked Ethel to tell me about the breakdown that really did scare Momma. Ethel told the story with details I had not heard before.

"It was so terrible, Annie. It was the time we all found out that Caroline was breakable. I was glad you were already in Washington. Marie was just a toddler when it happened. She cried most days for weeks. I think she knew our world was shaken.

"Every morning as the sun was rising, Caroline went to the barn to see Sadie and to make sure all the barn animals were fed. That day was no different. Being with the animals seemed to calm her. When something made her mad, she would go to the barn.

"I was helping Momma get dressed for the day. She had trouble with buttons.

"We heard a frightened whinny from Sadie. The pigs were squealing and then there was the crackling sound of wood burning. When Momma and I got around to the back of the house and could see where the noise was coming from, we both screamed. Caroline was holding tight to Sadie's bridle inside the burning barn. Caroline's shirt was pulled down from her shoulders. Her pants were ripped and her hair was a mess. The barn was on fire. The flames were taller than Sadie. Because Caroline was holding her so tightly, Sadie could not run. She was bucking and making all kinds of scared noises. Caroline stood frozen with her back to Sadie, chanting over and over in a calm voice, "It's okay. We are going to be all right. The Nash girls are always fine."

"I ran faster than Momma, so I got to Caroline first. I grabbed her shoulders and shook her. I was screaming at her 'You gotta get out of here! Let go of Sadie!' She wouldn't drop the bridle. Sadie was going crazy. She raised her front legs higher than I've ever seen before and brought them down on Caroline. The blow landed on Caroline's back between the shoulders. Caroline slammed face down in the ground and didn't move. Momma opened the barn doors wide so all the animals could get out. That created a bigger firestorm. The yellow and orange fire slapping the rafters of the roof looked like hell on earth. I yelled at Momma to go back to the house. Sadie went running, still bucking and whinnying. The other animals scattered anywhere they could find calm outside the barn.

"I grabbed Caroline's arms above her elbows and pulled her deadweight away from the barn. I was able to get her close to the house before I fell backwards. Her head landed in my lap. Neighbors came from all around to help. At that point though, all we could do was watch hellfire take away our barn."

While Ethel described the scene, I pulled the car off the road, screeching to a stop. I turned to face her as she was telling the horrific story. I was sick to my stomach. My hands were shaking. Dianne leaned over and hugged me. "It's okay now, dear girl," she said softly as she stroked my hair.

Ethel had to finish the story. "As we all know, Caroline was hurt pretty bad. Our next door neighbor carried her in their car to the hospital in Greenville. She stayed there two weeks. After treating her burns and the injuries from Sadie, they began changing medication to pull

Caroline back into the real world. She had been unconscious for days. When she woke, she did not speak. She could only eat soft foods and make small movements with her fingers. The nurses exercised her muscles while she was in the bed and by the end of two weeks she could stand. The doctors advised Momma that Caroline should go to Dix Hill for long term care. The doctors all agreed that Caroline's recuperation from this trauma could be months or years, and possibly she would never fully recover. That is when we sent for you, Annie. We needed you to come help us decide what to do. You were a godsend because you already knew about what they might be able to do for Caroline at the State Hospital.

"You know we lost Sadie that day. Most of her backside was burned. One of the farmhands brought his gun and did what was necessary to put dear Sadie out of her misery."

Even though it was hard to hear all this, I still needed to know more. I dropped the bombshell and asked one question I had never asked. I asked if Caroline had started the fire, if she intentionally tried to kill herself and Sadie.

Ethel raised her eyebrows as she looked over at Dianne, signaling how she would answer that question. Ethel said, "We don't know for sure. Since Caroline's injuries were so bad, doctors kept her sleeping heavily. When she came to, she said nothing. I mean, did not use her voice. After a month at Dix Hill, Caroline began to talk but never about that day.

"With the barn in ashes, Momma decided we should have the land cleared. The sheriff would not allow it. His men were trying to uncover the reason the barn caught fire. They found more than we knew at the time. A dead body in the back of the barn. It seemed to be that of a young man."

I was putting it all together now. We might never know what happened in the barn with the young man, what made Caroline do what she did, but this was why she was admitted to Dix Hill. I remember she was officially under arrest. It is clear to me now that Dix Hill was the only place to take her. She was a danger to herself and others.

Our meeting with Jane Hines was set for ten o'clock in the hospital cafeteria. My hands were sweating even though it was a cold January day. I was looking forward to speaking with Jane, but I was not sure I wanted to hear what she had to say about Caroline. I passed my list of topics to discuss to Dianne and said, "You do it. I don't think I can."

Dianne looked at me with sympathy and replied, "Of course, Annie, of course. This will be a sad happy day for all of us. Sad to hear about Caroline. Happy to get our arms around her."

We had arranged for Marie to stay in the nursery while we visited. Someday I wanted Jane to meet Marie, but not now. Jane was dressed in a white dress cinched at the waistline, white flat shoes, and a white starched hat. Around her left arm was a band with the red cross painted on it. I had not seen her in uniform. She looked so official. She stood tall with shoulders firm as she approached us. But the smile was all Jane. I relaxed a bit at seeing that smile. Jane greeted my sisters with a firm handshake. She grabbed my shoulders and brought me in for a hug.

She started talking fast, "I apologize for the official

uniform, Annie. After our meeting I am filling in for someone who trains the new nurses. I have to look the part, I guess. Unfortunately, I only have thirty minutes, so let me tell you what I have learned about Caroline.

"Caroline was understandably distraught when they brought her here. They ran all kinds of tests on her, medically and mentally. Caroline would not talk to anyone, especially not me. I do want you to know that Caroline is in the best place she can be right now. The doctors are excellent in their field. The staff is efficient and kind. I am proud to say the nursing staff is one of the best in a hospital for the criminally insane."

I became rigid. Dianne stepped back as if she had been slapped.

Ethel spoke in a firm but calm voice. "She is not a criminal! It was an accident. Caroline just has trouble sometime."

Jane relaxed her body and touched my arm. "I am so sorry, ladies. I did not mean to imply . . . Caroline is your sister and needs mental help. The state placed her in custody in a section of this facility that is called that. Please forgive my awful choice of words."

Dianne said, "I understand. What can you tell us about Caroline's ability to get well?"

"Caroline has a long road ahead of her. Everyone here wants her to get well. They have a plan which will include all kinds of therapy to improve her mind, body, and spirit. I know from Annie that you are a strong family. That will help. Follow the doctor's advice, and you will be able to help her heal."

My sisters and I listened as Jane talked to us about the mind and how it affects all parts of the body. And how a weakened body affects the mind. Dianne said, "Thank you, Jane, for explaining all this to us. We are more ready to meet her doctor now." Ethel just turned and walked away. Jane attempted to give me another hug, but I could not. It was all too depressing.

Ethel led us toward the office of one of the doctors. A man dressed in white pants and shirt stepped toward us before we got to Dr. Redmond's office. By the look on Ethel's face, we knew he was not Dr. Redmond. He said, "Hello, I am Doctor Alderman. I am afraid Dr. Redmond is unavailable. He asked me to speak with you on his behalf." He told us that Caroline had relapsed. Her mental state was in regression, and they had to move her back into the hospital last night. He said they were working to adjust her meds, so we would not be able to visit her after all. The scariest thing he told us was that Caroline was reporting that voices were telling her to hurt people again, so they had placed her in isolation.

When I explained that our mother had died, and we wanted to tell Caroline in person and wanted to see if she could come back with us to attend our mother's funeral, the doctor was adamant. He told us Caroline was in no condition to hear or accept her mother's death right now. He added that the hospital was trying to keep her and the other patients safe. He said Dr. Redmond would send us a report as soon as he could to let us know when we could see Caroline.

We drove the whole way back home without talking to one another. I turned on the radio, and we listened to jazz and pretended we hadn't heard that news.

MARCH 1932

Dianne
Settling Momma's Estate

Momma died two months after Dr. Walker diagnosed her with cancer. She evidently had been living with it for months, if not a year. Now Dianne, Annie, and I gathered to talk about how to cope with losing our mother. We had to settle the estate as well as decide what to do about Caroline. I have to say handling all the things necessary to settle our mother's estate put a strain on the Nash sisters' relationships. Conversations revealed heartbreak, anger, and even a little silliness. Dianne shares the memories and conversations she recalls when we were reminded that family love and responsibility loom larger than each of our own desires.

I could tell Ethel was getting angry, not only because she was shouting but also because she was letting the curse words fly. She shouted, "Jesus! I don't understand why this has to be so dang complicated! It is really not an estate. Estates are what son-of-a-gun RICH people have to settle."

Annie jumped right in, but on the opposite side of this debate. Her voice was also raised. "Don't be foolish, Ethel. All this has to be divided equally among Momma's daughters! And we have to figure out how to pay for Caroline's care! We must account for every dime!"

Ethel was not having any of that. She fired back, "Wait a dang minute! Do you think Caroline gets a fourth *and* her hospital costs? No way! We all will walk away with housing costs, especially me! This was my home. Once we sell, Marie and I have no place to live."

That quieted Annie down but she brought her stern face within inches of Ethel's and through gritted teeth said, "Stop yelling at me, Ethel! We will get nowhere unless we can speak like civilized people."

I had to break up the tension, so I started singing *America the Beautiful*. We Nash girls often sang to ourselves to relieve stress or anger.

O beautiful for spacious skies . . .

Annie and Ethel looked at me like I was crazy. But I kept on singing.

God shed His grace on thee . . .

Ethel said, "Jeez Louise, leave God out of this!" She was trying to hide a smile behind her grumpiness. Annie breathed deeply and shook her head. I brought my voice to its loudest volume for

from sea to shining sea.

We never knew anything but the first verse, but we often sang it when spring arrived at the farm. I wasn't sure this would cheer them up, but it got them to shut up for a bit. Ethel and Annie both stared at me. After a couple of silent minutes, they realized what I was trying to do.

Annie said, "Okay, Dianne, if we promise to calm down, will you stop singing?" They broke into a fit of laughter while I tried to act like someone had slapped my face. I couldn't hold the act very long and joined in their amusement.

I poured three glasses of sweet tea and said, "Let's go sit in the family room. We need to remember how much love we have for each other. Ethel, can Marie join us with her toys?"

The family room was not used unless we had company. It was a special place for us as girls because most of the time the door was closed. Maybe we could talk like family instead of enemies in that room. There is nothing like having Marie with us to change our attention to what is good in life. Marie entered the room holding Annie's hand. Ethel brought in a blue child's tea set for Marie. Over in one corner of the room were her fabric dolls and a doll bed with a blanket. I stared for a moment with heaviness in my heart. I knew Momma had made all those for Marie. There was also a child-sized wooden chair and table that I remembered Joseph, one of the farm workers, made for Marie.

"Look, Marie, we're going to have tea together," said Annie. "This is so nice. Thank you, Ethel. Thank you, Dianne. This feels more like our family."

In her youthful excitement, Marie went bounding

over to her table and grabbed one of her dolls to sit in her lap. "Yeah, Marie, we are gonna be nice," Ethel said only a little sarcastically.

Ethel sat in a wooden rocking chair made of walnut. It fit her body. We all knew where this chair came from, and it was ironic how secure Ethel looked sitting there. It was Frank's gift to her for, as he described it, birthing their child. He brought it by the house five days after Marie was born. At that time, Ethel still believed they would be married soon. It was a happy time that soon turned into sadness.

Annie admired the tea set and asked where it came from. She said she had seen them in D.C. They were called Lusterware and were made in Japan.

"The Pollards sent it to Marie for Christmas," Ethel admitted. "At first, I did not want to keep it, but she went nuts when we opened the package that had come in the mail. I figured there was no harm. She doesn't know them. She only gets to play with it on special occasions."

After a few minutes of quietly watching Marie be so gentle with the beautiful set, drinking from one cup and feeding her doll with another, Ethel got us started on the subject we needed to discuss. "I talked to the lawyer that helped me with the Frank mess. He will be happy to tie up the loose ends of Momma's things. He said we need to agree on what to sell and what to keep in the family. He also said he could represent Caroline at Dix Hill for however long she will live there. Any problems with letting him take care of the legal part of this? We have to pay him, of course. But that can come from the sale of anything before we split the money."

We all agreed that seemed to be the best thing since

none us of knew how to do any of that.

Annie remembered to ask the most important question. "Ethel, I don't think we ever asked if you wanted to sell the house and farm. I am sorry we did not. As you said, this is your home."

I started to answer for Ethel because we had talked about this, but Ethel spoke quickly. "I don't want to live here. This is not really my house, it's Momma's. When Marie was born, my plan was to get married and move away with Frank. You know that story. Frank wanted his parents' money more than he wanted me. I stayed here to help Momma, and she liked having Marie close by. Now that Momma is gone, I couldn't stand to be here seeing her in every corner of this house and land and know she's not here. I need a new life for Marie and me. The sale of all this will make it possible for us to do that."

Annie reminisced a moment. "I know what you mean, Ethel. When I see the swing out front and the fence that will be covered in yellow roses, it makes make me sad. The Virginia Creeper, that red vine beside the porch, now looks sorrowful to me. Remember when we used to climb that vine to get up on the roof? We could see the whole county up there. That vine was like us sisters. Changing every season. Growing green leaves in the spring and a stronger trunk in the summer. Then turning red in the fall before dropping its leaves. It hung there waiting to come back to life after winter. And then the flat land where the barn used to be. It is all too gloomy to stay around. Dianne, how about you?"

"This morning I was sitting on the front porch with

my coffee and a black car went by and paused in front of the house. I just stared at it. A sharp memory came alive. It was almost as if time stopped that day the Army came to tell us that Daddy was killed in the war. Caroline was in Lila's arms when Momma fell apart. Ethel, do you remember Lila?" Ethel nodded.

Dianne continued, "She was so easy with Caroline. I think Lila was the reason Caroline wanted to take care of children. That memory struck me in the gut this morning like someone punched me. I felt sick. At that point I knew it was the right thing to sell. Ethel is right. She usually is."

By the end of the week we had written a list of everything we wanted to sell and each of us had our own list of what we wanted to take with us. We decided the house with the ten acres could be sold separately from the ninety acres of farmland. Since the crash in 1929, farming was a terrible way to make a living, but maybe someone would buy it with hopes of things getting better. Thank goodness Momma had been sensible with her money. She only owed the bank for last year's seeds. There was no mortgage on the land. Momma never borrowed money to pay the farm workers. She paid them out of her savings every year.

On Friday, March 18, 1932, the Nash sisters, except for Caroline, signed the legal papers to settle the estate of Florence Nash. The lawyer signed for Caroline, as he was authorized to do. After more discussion we had agreed to divide any money we got from the sale of property four ways. If we did not make enough money for a fourth to cover Caroline's medical bills, we would divide the money differently. Annie insisted that she didn't need the money. She had a good job, paid her rent easily, and there were men around willing to buy her what else she might need.

Joe had a secure job at the mill, and I made money raising vegetables and sewing for other families. If need be, whatever was earned from the sale of the farm would be used to get Ethel settled in a new place and pay for Caroline's care at Dix Hill.

The following week we packed up what we wanted from the house. Annie's car was big enough for her to carry all her things back to Washington. Joe came from Burlington with a horse and wagon big enough to take what was on my list. Ethel would stay in the house as long as she needed to. We hoped she would take time to find the right house for her little family. We set a date to come back in the summer. Most likely it would take several months for anything to sell. It would be our excuse to help her pack up the rest of the dishes, linens, and furniture, and we could try again to visit Caroline.

As we stood in the front yard for one more goodbye, I decided to tell them my news. "I read somewhere that when a person dies another one is born. Well, that might be true. Joe and I are finally going to have a baby! If all goes well, Marie will have a cousin at the end of the summer."

Tears trailed from Annie's eyes. I couldn't tell if they were happy or sad tears. She grabbed my shoulders and pulled me to her. "Oh, Dianne, this is so wonderful! I am happy beyond words for you and Joe!"

Ethel said, "Woo boy. What a load you will have on your hands! Those ladies in mill town are going to want to take over for you! They will boss you around in all new ways."

She paused, then joined the Nash girl hug. "I guess I am gonna have to live closer to you so Marie will know her cousin. Hey, Joe, you got enough room in that house for all of us?"

Joe yelled back from the wagon, "I think if you are all coming, we've got to find a bigger house!"

I put my arm around Annie and walked her to the car. "Would you come too? Would you live with us?"

Drying her tears through a smile she said, "We'll see. I am not sure I could find a good job in Burlington and certainly won't find rich men! But we will see."

As Annie got into her car, Ethel started belting out a song to the tune of America the Beautiful. She obviously had practiced it a few times, but not many.

How beautiful the Nash girls are,
With family waves of love,
For moving away from memories
To new ones that we'll love!
Nash Girls! Oh, Nash Girls!
Let's shed our grace on thee
And crown ourselves with sisterhood
From D.C. to Raleigh!

Annie backed her car around to leave but paused to hear the song. Joe and I pulled ourselves up on the packed wagon. I shouted as tears were pouring, "Sing it one more time, Ethel! I want to have it on my mind all the way home!"

So Ethel belted it out once more.

How beautiful the Nash girls are,
With family waves of love,
For moving away from memories
To new ones that we'll love!
Nash Girls! Oh, Nash Girls!
Let's shed our grace on thee
And crown ourselves with sisterhood
From D.C. to Raleigh!

After the encore ended, Annie started to drive away. She flung her arm out the window and waved goodbye.

APRIL 1932

Ethel
Visiting Caroline

Dianne and Annie came back home a month later. They wanted to help me organize any furniture we did not want so it could be sold. But more importantly, we were going to visit Caroline.

Finding out about Caroline's life and treatment at Dorothea Dix State Hospital had brought sadness and happiness. Caroline must live there until she is no longer diagnosed as insane. We knew this was the best option for Caroline, given what happened at home. No matter how beautiful the campus was or how kind and effective the doctors and nurses were, Caroline was in prison.

Here is how the Nash sisters made it through the visit.

As we drove through the gates in Annie's fancy car, we got lots of stares from people wandering around the property. Annie held her arm out the window of that big, green Nash car, waving and yelling, "Hello!" Hey y'all!" to nearly everyone we passed. They waved back with big smiles like they were seeing famous people riding by in a parade.

We had been told to go to the hospital first and talk with Caroline's doctor and nurses. They were expecting us. Even though all three of us had been there before, the hospital struck me as bigger than any building I had ever seen. I said, "Geez, I wonder how many people stay in there." Annie turned around to me and said, "Too many."

There was a woman at a small desk in the front lobby. She was talking on the phone to someone, so we waited. The ceilings were high. There were tall windows, but each one had iron bars covering it. I saw Dianne move close to Annie and ask her if she was doing okay. Annie looked so sad and said, "No. I hate this place. It smells like nothing and no one. Like there is no life here. I despise that Caroline lives here."

Dianne hugged Annie and said, "I agree, Annie. It smells clean. Too clean. Like they are covering up something."

I moved close to my sisters and whispered, "I don't wish this on Caroline, but she needs help and this seems like the only place where she can get it."

We all jumped a little when the woman behind the desk asked if she could help us.

We walked over to her, and I said, "Yes. We are sisters of Caroline Nash. We want to visit her but are supposed to see her doctor first. Can we go back? We've been here before."

In a very patient tone the woman replied, "Yes, of course, you can see Caroline. Caroline is in the arts and crafts room on the fourth floor. Someone will have to escort you there. The doctor will be down this hallway." She was pointing behind her. "Go through those doors. Caroline's doctor and caregivers are waiting for you in room 135."

None of us could smile. It seemed all happiness was pulled from our bodies. Annie, the ever polite, managed to say thank you as we walked toward the doors.

We grabbed each other's hand and walked down the long hallway like Dorothy and her friends in the *Wizard of Oz* movie that we had all seen. Room 135 seemed a mile away.

I knocked on the door and a man's voice called out, "Enter!" Standing behind a desk was the same man Momma and I met when we came the first time. He was tall but slumped and used a cane to get around the desk. "Welcome, I am so glad you are here."

I pointed to myself then to each of my sisters and said, "I am Ethel. This is my sister Dianne and my sister Annie. We have been here together before but could not see Caroline because she was not doing well. I hope there is better news this time."

He smiled and shook each of our hands and said, "I'm Doctor Tom Redmond. You can call me Doc. These people over here are most important to you. They take good care of Caroline. This is Belle Parker." He pointed to a large black woman with the warmest smile. Belle came over, put her hand on each of our shoulders, one at a time, and held it there just a moment. With that kind smile, she said, "I am so glad to know you. Every one of you."

Doc said, "She is a caregiver. She knows Caroline like a friend. And here is Caroline's nurse, Mrs. Sandra Quinn."

Mrs. Quinn looked like someone that didn't want us to call her Sandra. She just nodded her head in an official type of move and said, "Good to meet you."

We all sat down at a large round table, and Doc began to talk.

"First let me say how sorry I am that you lost your mother. She was such a dear person. She wanted the best treatment for Caroline. I want to summarize a few things. As you know, Caroline has been here a year. She was brought here by her own choice. She was transported here from the hospital where they cared for her physical wounds following the fire. When the authorities charged her with a crime, the result of the judicial process was that the state required her to be here. Caroline was not convicted of arson or murder by reason of insanity. As her doctor, I concurred with the decision for Caroline to be confined here until she is well. Our job is to care for Caroline's mental wounds."

I could hear Annie begin to cry softly.

He continued, "Prior to the authorities making their decision about Caroline, your mother made arrangements for her to be treated for another year. Now Caroline's cost of care is being covered by the State of North Carolina. You will be able to pick up a check for the balance owned the estate of Florence Nash from the clerk before you leave."

At that, we were all reaching for our handkerchiefs. Dianne dabbed her eyes. She had something important on her mind. "Dr. Redmond, will Caroline's care and treatment be the same as if we are paying for it? I don't want her to get less attention because the government cannot afford it."

"Dianne, I don't know much about budget or bookkeeping, but I can assure you we treat each patient based on what they need. Not what it will cost."

Belle spoke as if she was hurt. "You can count on that! Caroline is not a case number; she is a person we care about! I know we can help her. I have already seen some healing of her heart. I know there will also be more healing of her mind."

Dianne quickly responded saying she was sorry, but she just wanted to be sure.

"I know you did. It is okay." Belle said with that warm smile back in place.

It seemed Doc needed to change the subject. "Yes. No need for anyone to apologize. Now, Mrs. Quinn, can you explain Caroline's condition and treatment?"

"Certainly, Doctor," the nurse said. "Caroline is psychosomatic, meaning she has a disorder of the mind. She has erratic emotions, suffers bouts of depression, claims she hears voices telling her to hurt people, and is paranoid.

"In the first few months she was here, she did not socialize with others and did not feel safe anywhere but in her room. The doctors prescribed medication to balance her moods and quiet the voices. The therapies we used were slow integration with others here and assigning her chores that were rhythmic in nature such as folding towels and washing dishes. The doctors adjusted medications, and we monitored her food intake.

We began an exercise regimen twice a week. When it became apparent that Caroline was very good with her hands, we let her work in the garden.

"Belle, can you talk about Annie's temperament?"

Belle stood as she talked, "Of course, Nurse Quinn. Do you ladies have any questions so far? I know it is a lot to take in."

All three of us shook our heads. I wanted to learn Belle's perspective. Everything from Mrs. Quinn was too clinical for me. I said, "Not at this time. Please, Belle, tell us what you think of Caroline."

Belle said, "Caroline is a strong person about to become a young woman. She has suffered a lot that we still don't know about. She is working very hard to get better. Last night when I told her goodnight, she asked if I thought she could behave when you all came. I went to her bed, gave her a big hug, and said, 'Yes. But I know your sisters will want you just as you are.' I say that just so you know how much she wants to heal.

"Caroline is particular about how she does things. If she is pulling weeds, she will make sure each plant has room to breathe. She will work hours on that. And she checks on them every day. Caroline said she can't hear voices when she is working hard.

"Caroline likes children. I saw in her chart that she was a babysitter before coming here, so I took her to visit the child nursery we have here. She was the happiest I've ever seen her with the preschool children. They feel easy with her. Lots of hugs and laughter happened in that short visit. With permission from Nurse Quinn and Dr. Redmond, we are going to assign her to the nursery as her full time job. I know she will be happy when I tell her. Actually, why don't you all tell her and find out why she likes it so much."

Annie interrupted, "I know why she likes it. She is careful and sweet with children. She once said to me that 'Children don't care whether I am odd. They don't even notice.' I thank you so much for finding out what works for Caroline."

Dianne wanted to leave. "Can we see her now? I really need to see my sister."

Doc stood and said, "Certainly. We can talk more later if you like. We just want you to feel assured that Caroline is in good hands."

Again came the tears. All three sisters and Belle.

Belle escorted us to the arts and crafts room to see Caroline. There she was in a large room at a table folding napkins. We just watched her from the other side of the room for a few moments. Caroline was thin, way too thin. Her color was not good. There was a yellowish tint to her skin. Her hair was clean and styled, but the color was dull. Caroline always had the prettiest hair in the family. A chestnut color with a beautiful shine to it. She was the only sister that really brushed her hair 100 strokes like Momma told us all to do. Caroline looked older than 16. Her life had already been too hard.

Annie walked over to Caroline and called her name softly, "Hi, Caroline, it's me, Annie."

"I know who you are. They told me you were coming. Where is the rest of my so called family?"

Dianne approached singing a song we've sung a thousand times together since she was a little girl.

Caroline used to call it the silly word song.

As soon as we realized what Dianne was doing, we began singing with her. We knew this by heart.

Skid-dy-mer-rink-a-dink-a-boomp,
Skid-dy-mer-ink-a-doo means I love you.
Skid-dy-mer-rink-a-dink-a-boomp,
Skid-dy-mer-rink-a-doo means I'll be true.
Skid-dy-mer-rink-a-doo-a-boomp,
Skid-dy-mer-rink-a-doo,

Caroline looked up at us and turned that frown into a smile and joined us in song. Only she changed the last line of the song for her.

Skid-dy-mer-rink-a-doo-a-boomp,
Skid-dy-mer-rink-a-doo, means you love me!

Caroline stopped abruptly and looked around at everyone staring at us. We were the only noise in the place, so we came in with a big finish. As we always did, we pointed to Caroline as we sang her favorite line.
Skid-dy-mer-rink-a-doo means I'll be true.

When we stopped singing there was some laughter. Belle started the clapping in the back of the room with the caregivers joining in. Quickly the others in the room began to clap quite energetically.

Caroline stood and took a bow. Then came the Nash sisters hug. It felt like family again!

We talked for hours about home, childhood, the men in our lives, and Annie's car. No one brought up anything negative. I could tell Caroline was working hard to stay focused. Annie decided we should go for a walk outside. Caroline looked over at Belle.

Belle jumped right in with her sweet voice. "That is a wonderful idea! Caroline, you can go with your sisters. I don't need to go with you. Take them to the picnic tables under the big oak tree. They will like that."

Caroline was humming our song as we approached the front porch steps down to the grass. Annie placed her arm in the crook of Caroline's arm and I took Caroline's other arm while Dianne linked with me. We took the steps down raising our knees high like we were in a marching band, humming all the way.

When we reached the picnic table, someone brought over tomato and mayonnaise sandwiches, pickles, and glasses of sweet tea.

While we were eating, Dianne broached the subject of Dix Hill with Caroline. She said, "Caroline, this is such a lovely place. Do you like it here?"

Caroline stared at her hands and responded slow and measured. "I guess. I don't have a lot of choice, do I? The people are nice here. And Belle reminds me of Momma—except she is black. They give me jobs to do that keep me busy so I can push back the bad thoughts."

She raised her eyes to us then pointed beyond the tree to a huge vegetable garden. Caroline's voice became more rapid and excited. "You see that? I work over there every day. That looks like our garden at home. Only gigantic. You all taught me how to take care of a garden. Momma always said the weeding is the worst part but the most important. I am the fastest weed puller anyone has ever seen! And I know what to pull and what not to pull. Most girls don't know the difference."

I wanted to keep her talking and focused on the good things. "It is a fine garden, Caroline. We hear you liked your visit to the child nursery. Tell us about that."

She began to sound like our little sister. She always was a talker, except when she was worried about something. "It is the cutest place you've ever seen! There are three rooms. One for babies, one for walking babies, and a bigger one for preschool children. All the rooms are painted with pretty colors and have curtains that blow softly through the open windows. Ethel, it reminds me of how you fixed up your room for baby Marie. The nursery has child sized furniture and plenty of toys. It is such a good place for children to be. Those children didn't have much of a life until they came here. Even though their mom or dad has to be here because they are crazy, the children have a good place to stay during the day. Isn't that marvelous?"

OCTOBER 1935

Dianne
Conversations While Waiting

Some of the best conversations happen while waiting at the hospital or spending time with people who need your companionship for long periods of time. In these circumstances topics do not end; they morph into the next topic, and you come back to topics time and time again to extend what else you remember. Shared memories expose unexpected perspectives and often new understanding. Dianne talks about what happened on those days in October 1935 when I spent time with her at Richardson Memorial Hospital.

I heard Ethel enter the ward where I was hospitalized like a bull busting out of the pen to chase a young heifer. She was huffing and puffing. She said, "Dianne, it took me so long time to find this hospital. I hate that I was not here to bring you in. How are you? What happened?"

I told her to settle down so I could tell her about

it, then I explained about falling off the back porch at home and yelling loud enough a neighbor heard me. Dale, who lives next door, came running over. I had hurt my leg by falling against the bottom stone step, and I hit my head on something so blood was pouring out. That is what scared Dale. She got two other neighbors to pull a car into the yard and drag me into the car. They brought me here because Dale said it is the oldest hospital in the area. By oldest I am hoping she meant best.

Ethel calmed down a bit, put her pocketbook beside me on the bed, and pulled the curtains between me and the others in the room. Then she plopped down in the wooden chair beside my bed and said she didn't understand why oldest made this place better than others. She lowered her voice and whispered, "There are nine other beds in here with you. They can't have enough nurses to look after you and all those people. How are they treating you?"

For the next hour or so, I told Ethel the story of rushing out the backdoor because I thought I saw Joe standing outside. I see Joe sometimes in my dreams or just when I am being really quiet. I don't think I am crazy. I just think he is reassuring me. He came again this morning. There he was, clear as day, standing in the backyard, leaning on his shovel. He held his hat in his hand and wiped the sweat from his forehead with the back of his arm. He was looking right at me. I opened the screen door to see him more clearly. He tipped his head down a bit, smiled, and winked at me. Joe would do this before he would lean over and kiss me. I closed my eyes and felt the warmth of his lips on my cheek. It felt wonderful. So, I ran to him. That's when I tripped and fell hard on the ground. I looked around to see if he was still there. I needed him to come help me get up. I didn't see him so I began calling out. I called him real loud and that's when Dale came running.

Ethel just shook her head.

I went on to tell her the doctor said he thinks my leg is broken. It's wrapped up for now, and they are going to X-ray it this afternoon. If the leg is broken bad, they will have to do surgery to put it back together. I'm not sure what to think about that. At least my head is fine, just a cut they stitched up.

Just as I was finishing up my story, a nurse came to check on me. Ethel gave her the third degree about her training, how she could care for this many people at once, and then the all too common Nash family questions came. "Who are your people? Where did you grow up?"

I never understood those questions from our family because our relations were nothing to brag about.

The nurse answered all Ethel's questions. Turns out she is from Forsyth county and her people are Moravians who have been here for generations. That seemed to be respectable enough for Ethel. She said, "I don't know any Moravians, but I understand you are religious folk. I like that. I am not so religious anymore, but it's good for a nurse to be."

The nurse stepped back saying, "Nice to meet you, Ethel. Your sister is going to need lots of rest to heal. When she gets sleepy, let her have peace and quiet. Okay?"

After the nurse left, I told Ethel I would let her know when I needed a nap, but right now, I wanted to talk.

Being in this hospital bed had given me some time to think. I said to her, "I am glad you are here. We have a lot to talk about."

Then I started and hardly stopped to take a breath or a sip of water. Ethel interrupted from time to time.

I was reading a book with Suzy recently.

Ethel stopped me almost mid-sentence. "Oh, by the way George is going to be at your house when the school bus comes. He will have them drop off Marie too and bring both girls over to our house until you can come home."

I knew they would get things arranged for me, and said, "Thanks to you and George for doing that."

I brought her back to what I wanted to talk to her about. The story book I was reading was *The Little Engine That Could*. It's a child's book, but I kept thinking it related well to the Nash Girls. I told Ethel if she hadn't read it to Marie, she could borrow it from my house. I told her not to laugh because I wanted her to read a children's book. Ethel snickered when I told her the author's name was Watty Piper. She said that was a name he should have changed before writing a book.

I ignored that and went on with what I was trying to explain to her. I told her the story was one that makes children feel hopeful—to believe in themselves. It also made me feel hopeful and thankful.

The story is about a happy train engine pulling cars full of fun things for children. The engine's job is to deliver the toys, dolls, teddy bears, healthy food, and many other things to children on the other side of the mountain. Then one day the train broke down and couldn't make it over the mountain. He knew without the good things he was carrying for girls and boys, well, they would have no toys to play with and no wholesome food to eat. He could not get over the mountain. Another engine came to help him, then another and another. Once they all worked together chanting, "I think I can – I think I can – I think I can," they did it. They got to the other side of the mountain.

I could see Ethel was not taking this seriously and not getting my point. Okay, it was sounding a little silly as I was telling it. We both started laughing and could not stop. If felt like a Nash sister moment.

Right then lunch was delivered, so we had to act grown-up. Ethel inspected the food and said, "That looks pretty healthy, Dianne. Tomorrow I will bring you country ham and red-eye gravy. Maybe I'll throw in some collards. We have to keep feeding you what your body is used to. This stuff might make you sick." We laughed again.

After lunch, I was surprised to find I needed a nap. When I woke, Ethel was by my bed. She said that while I was "out like a light" she went to a find a telephone to update George. I started right back on the point I wanted to make. I grabbed her hand and said, "Ethel, here is the point of me telling you about that book. The little train engine needed help to get over the mountain. That is true of us. Suzy and I have needed help, but we don't always like to ask for it. It has been over a year since Joe died in that accident at the mill. You know this has not been an easy year for Suzy and me. Neither of us is doing well without him. This load that we carry seems too large.

"It just happened that Suzy brought that book home from school. The youngest children were reading it. She and I read it together one night a few weeks ago. The first time we read it, we cried like babies about those poor children across the mountain. Suzy said to me, 'We would help wouldn't we, Momma? Even though we don't have Papa and we don't have an engine, we would help.'

"It struck me like lightning. Of course, we would! We would stick together. We have always gotten through things that were hard. She and I have read that book every night before bed. It is our reminder that we think we can get through this and whatever else comes. Then I realized that the Nash sisters do the same thing. We pull together when it counts, and we think we can handle anything that comes along.

"I began thinking about all the men in our lives. They don't seem to stay long, but they bring important things to us. Joe was the best thing that ever happened to me. He taught me how to love, reminded me to be kind, and to organize my life. Joe is the one that talked, all the time, about making a plan and sticking to it. It seemed when he died, there was no need for a plan. I would just let life happen.

"Ethel, you have good men in your life. Even though you and Frank never worked it out between you, he has given you so much. Even without being able to marry you, stay with you, or be in Marie's life, he provided for you. I know he broke your heart. But you learned to move on. Ethel, you are the strongest of all of us— although you were not Momma's favorite—that was me." We both smiled.

"Then Larry came along. What an interesting man! He thought you were the bee's knees! You wanted to marry him real quick at the court house. I knew getting married then would be too soon. It seemed like a rebound from Frank. Then the crash of '29 happened. I'm not telling you anything you don't know, but I want to say this part. It is important. Larry had been doing well in his insurance sales work, but, as you told us, he did not do well when the stock market crashed. He wanted to provide for you and Marie, and I could tell he loved you. But remember he left. He was sincere about coming back when he made enough money. He said he was heading out to Alabama."

Ethel put her hand on my arm to interrupt. "Yeah, Larry was an interesting man. He had worldly ideas. He always wanted to be something more. He told me getting married would give me and Marie the security we needed. Later he disappeared. Larry figured he could build another office just like he did in Atlanta. He said Alabama was the right place because those people were hard working and needed insurance. They didn't lose money in the crash because they didn't use banks and had no money in the stock market. It all seemed to make sense to me. I never promised to go with him. Or counted on him coming back. That way I would not be disappointed. I just told him 'I'll see you around maybe.'"

"Yes, I remember, Ethel. What did Larry bring you? We can talk more about this later, but hear me out. I think he brought you a view of what you could be. You managed without Frank because you were mad at him. With Larry you became an independent woman because you found out you could. And you were good at it. Larry traveled so much, you learned more about the world out there. Since he was not always around, you stopped depending on him and started liking who you were. You began to be not only a mom but also a farm owner and business woman. Marie was not just a duty. She was a gift from God. Okay that might be a little too sappy. But this is the time in your life you began to understand that."

Ethel piped in, "I thank goodness for Larry, mainly because he didn't stay long. And maybe I will see him again."

"Then in 1934 when George Fox stepped off a wagon at home asking for a job, you said "yes." Not only did you need help with the house, but you needed a family. I am not sure you see this, but George is the one who has shown Marie what a papa could be," I reminded her.

Ethel and I talked for the two days I was at Richardson Memorial Hospital about the men in our lives. Us growing up without a papa. How strong our momma was to raise four girls by herself. The challenges of life in general and how we are doing just fine. We talked about our daughters and how close they are. The Nash girls never had any cousins. We just had each other. Ethel and I agreed that Suzy and Marie having each other was adding to their happiness. The longest part of our continued conversation was that men were nice to have around when they were good to us, but they were not necessary for surviving.

Ethel said it best. "We women have all the smarts we need to accomplish anything we want." Now we need to be smart enough to know when to ask for help.

1940

Nash Sisters
The Nash Round-Robin Letters

Things are really different for the Nash family. The Nash Round-Robin letters go to fewer sisters now. But we still write as a journal or history of the family. I share about the visits from Frank. Caroline uses humor to talk about her life at the insane asylum. Annie shines a light on living in D.C. and, of course, on politics.

To the Nash Women that are left to read my letter – October 4, 1940

What a year this has been! I think I need everyone's pages to get through telling you all that is happening to me and Marie. It seems like forever since we were in the same room together, but that is the way our life is now. Thank you, Annie, for coming down for Dianne's funeral and helping me organize her property.

Caroline, we missed you there. I am glad you had visited Dianne in the hospital a few months back. Belle was so good to take you there. I know that was hard on you, but Dianne's smile told the whole story. She appreciated it. Caroline, remember what I said about these letters. When you are reading them, if there comes a point that gets you all nervous and upset—stop reading. When I visit you, I can tell you all the good news so you don't have to go through the sad stuff.

Dianne was so organized. She spent time before she last went into the hospital putting stuff in boxes by category. She remembered Momma's file system which made it easier for us. The most precious box of all held the legal papers giving permission for George and me to adopt Suzy. She and George kept that from me, so I learned it the same time as Marie and Suzy. Boy did I cry my eyeballs out when I heard that! I can't imagine another gift in the world better than that. I hope when I go, I will have taken care of everything as well as Dianne did.

Speaking of dying. The final medical report said that Dianne died of cancer. I kind of knew that. It did not matter much, except that is one more on the books for the BIG C.

Marie and Suzy have enjoyed being together. Once we got everything situated with Dianne and Joe's house, we set up a bedroom for the two girls to share at our place. They refused to have separate bedrooms. Suzy said she did not ever want to sleep alone again. Marie totally agreed, saying neither of them was an only child anymore. Their room is bright and sunny. I made bedspreads and curtains to match. The fabric I used is blue with tuffs of cotton threads sticking up in an orderly way. I think the magazines call it chenille. I put a fringe border around the bottom. Although Dianne was better at sewing than me, I think she would approve.

George's job as a car mechanic is going well. Since the depression people are not buying new cars; they want to fix the ones they have. George is good at it. He says he can fix anything from bumper to bumper. We are doing well. I am just tending to the garden and the house. I also spend a lot of time keeping two girls out of trouble.

Caroline, the last time I visited, you were not feeling well. The doctors said you caught something going around. I hope by now you are back to normal. I get scared of most medical words—cancer, flu, polio, tuberculosis. The doctor said he is pretty sure you have none of the bad ones. You just might be feeling sluggish. He said rest and plenty of good food would help. Please let us know how you are doing now.

Okay, here is the news that is causing the biggest problem. Frank keeps coming around. He says he is owed a chance to get to know Marie. He says he wants to provide for her. Thank God he only visits when Marie is at school. She doesn't know about him. All she knows about a loving father is George. No need for her to know anything else.

Each time Frank comes, he leaves money. At first it was just a few dollars and a small gift for Marie. I told him we did not need anything from him. We were fine on our own. But he won't quit coming. Sometimes he just leaves a letter with money in it. Other times I am home, and we have an argument about his "rights" as a father. I have been honest with George about Frank coming, and he told me I should tell the police about it. I said to George, "What am I going to tell them? There is a man bringing me money, make him stop!"

I'm not scared of Frank coming here. I'm just annoyed. Anyway, last week he came when I was not home but George was. They evidently got into a fight. I mean a real fight, 'cause George had a shiner. George said he thinks he convinced Frank, man-to-man, to stay away."

Frank evidently told George that he would not come back, but to give a letter to me. It was four pages long and made me mad and sad. Here is the gist of it.

Frank was making excuses why he had to go away when Marie was born. He said he was using the money his parents promised to make a "real life" for me and Marie. I've heard all that before. He went into some detail about being a lawyer and how successful he was. But he said, "I'll never be really happy until I make it all up to you and our little family can be together again."

Geez! He knows I am married to George, but said he would wait for me. Oh, good God. Sounds like that movie with Janet Gaynor and (somebody whose first name I can't remember) March in A Star is Born. I guess Frank wants to make me a star.

The sweet part of the letter was about Marie. He said he saw her from a distance at school and "E, she is beautiful. She was happy, laughing, and jumping rope with some girls. She will be a good athlete. They were chanting rhymes and counting. She was up to 100 jumps without stopping! And that hair, E! Her jet black curls looked just like you. She is as lovely as her mother." That part made me weep a bit because he is right about most of that. Marie is smart, kind, and loves to use her muscles in all kinds of games. I am proud of that child. You all know she fills my heart.

At the end of the letter he wrote the number of a bank account at a bank in Raleigh. He said the name on the account is Marie Nash but it is for both of us. He said until she is 18, I will have to sign to withdraw money for her. Frank has been putting money in that bank account since his parents died in a car crash in 1932. You guys remember, Mr. and Mrs. Pollard were coming home from a party and he crashed the car, killing them both. Somebody at the scene of the wreck said it was probably good Mr. Pollard was so drunk he never knew what happened because his wife was thrown from the car into a tree.

Anyway, Frank's letter said he inherited money from them and his law practice was doing well and he didn't need it all, so he put money in the account anytime he could. He signed the letter, "You and Marie should be very comfortable now. From the man who will always love you. Frank."

So sappy. I don't know how much is in there, but I will check the next time I go see you, Caroline.

I'll sign off. Can't wait for this round-robin letter to come 'round again.

I love you both,

Ethel, the oldest now

Hello sisters! — October 14, 1940

I just wanted to remind you that I am crazy, not stupid. I can read letters and know when to put them down. I take enough medicine to kill a cow, and they will give me more if they see me acting crazier. I stopped reading for a moment when Ethel talked about Dianne and again when she described the Pollards' crash. I don't think I ever heard that. Not sure what I thought happened to them but never knew it was a bloody mess.

Ethel, I perked up like a sane person when you talked about all the money you have. If you want,

I can go down to that bank in Raleigh and find out how much we/you have. If you could see me, you would see my devil face when I wrote that.

I push away thoughts of Dianne being gone from us. That is not too hard since I have not been around for years. The picture I want in my head is the young Dianne. There is that image of her bossing me around with that brown hair falling over her left eye as she gave me the look. I knew there was always a twinkle in her eye underneath those curls.

I am glad Marie and Suzy are living as sisters. No girl should grow up without sisters. Maybe even a brother too. Work on that, Ethel. You are not too old yet.

Annie, you just had another birthday! Happy day to you. If my mind still does arithmetic right, you are 27 years old. Geez, that is a lot of years! I hope you ate cake.

My doctors think I am doing okay. The spasms and fits have nearly stopped. I sleep a lot. Those brain shock treatments really help me. Some people hate them and say the pain is awful. But it doesn't hurt me. From the first one they did, my fits stopped, so I'll go as many times as they want me to.

And I still like my job in the nursery. The children are fun to play with. And they really like when I hold them, read a book to them, or make projects with them. Like most people, they like attention. These children with crazy parents don't get much attention paid to them except when they are here.

It seems like everyone in this place is sick. In the cafeteria you never heard such coughing and cussing.

But the cussing is normal. People cough and then cuss, like they were saying 'scuse me.

Many of my friends are sick. Especially the older ones. They don't come to the cafeteria anymore. They eat in their rooms. I guess that is to keep the cooties away from us or so they can sleep while being pumped with medicine. Last week three of my closest friends went to the hospital to stay. They had trouble breathing and coughed so much they could not eat or sleep. Doctors say the new medicine, penicillin, will help them get better. I hope it is the miracle medicine they say it is because I might get sick too.

To end this letter on a good note (like Dianne would want me to do), I want to tell you how much I appreciate you. I have done some bad things and caused a lot of trouble. But you all have stuck by me. You are good sisters. Just like Momma taught us to be.

Love, Caroline

Dear, dear sisters – October 23, 1940

Now we are three. As a family, we were six, then five when Daddy was killed in the war, four when Momma died and now three with Dianne gone. It makes me so sad. I have moments most days when I will see something that reminds me of family, and I break down and cry.

I am worried about being around crowds because I might catch something. And D.C. is full of people. Hordes of them. Since the crash in '29, homeless people are everywhere. Whole families are living on the streets, in the parks, and under bridges by the Potomac River. Even if they aren't sick, they look like they are. They scare me.

People are now beginning to find jobs. More government departments are hiring again. I am seeing new restaurants and shops opening or reopening since the crash. The Civilian Conservation Corps has been good to get the healthy back to work. I have friends whose husbands left for a job when the Corps expanded the age to include men up to 28 years old. It is not much money at $30 a month, but when they send $25 a month back home to their families, it really helps. President Roosevelt is a smart man to know his country needed the New Deal.

I am so lucky to have kept a job through all this. Part of the reason I have been lucky is that I am still single and have a government job. Married women who held government jobs in the last ten years had to quit so an unemployed man could be given the job. Moving from one government department to another has not been so bad. The work in a secretary pool is similar, no matter who is the boss. My last change was two months ago when I moved to the

War Department. I didn't want to go into that group because I don't like war and think we should not spend money on it. But I had no alternative when they shut down my last department. They don't ask your opinion; they just tell you to go to a new department or lose your job. Now I type letters for the generals. I am learning a lot, but it is all about how our men "fight for their country."

The best thing about this job is Jonathan Walsh. He is an advisor to General Summerall, who reports directly to the President. I met him when I started the new job, and he asked that I be assigned to his administrative group. He meets individually with each of his staff to let us know as much as he can about his responsibility and what we can do to help. I feel better working in the War Department if the work really matters. Mr. Walsh and I speak to each other daily. I sit right outside his office. He brings me coffee when he gets his. He is interested in me. Yesterday he said, "Miss Nash, if you don't mind me asking, why has a man not caught and married you?"

My answer was the same I tell everyone who asks this. "The right man hasn't tried hard enough." He chuckled and walked into his office.

I don't know if this "flirting" will ever turn into something, but if it does, I'll have to leave the job. They don't like men and women in the same office seeing each other. I have to get moving on this marriage thing. As Caroline reminded me, I am twenty-seven and single. A few more years and people will call me a spinster. I want a family so bad. Actually I want children. I need a man for that, at least in the beginning.

I am jealous of you, Ethel, for so many reasons. The first is Marie. What a wonderful child you have! And now Frank is paying up, literally, for being so neglectful. You will have your pockets stuffed with money. You can hire things done, which can help the economy. Tee hee.

And I am jealous that you were able to move to Burlington and be near Dianne and Suzy. You got there in the nick of time too. Dianne must have waited for you to get there before the Big C invaded her body. And now you have added Suzy to your family just like Dianne wished.

Caroline, I am sorry you have not been feeling well. It is great that you have doctors watching over you. The illnesses that are in the U.S. are prolific. I read in the newspaper that one in seven people has syphilis, and it can kill you. I wonder what Preacher Thomas at the Methodist church back home would say about that. We all know how you get that disease! We are safe from that one. We only have sex with clean men or our husbands. Right, girls??

Caroline, you should be safe from polio. I think that strikes children. But since we are not sure how that is spread, we should all be aware. And keep Marie and Suzy safe, Ethel. I have a friend who is a nurse at the hospital in D.C. She said the beds are full of people with pneumonia and influenza. She thinks it is because people are so poor they don't have enough food. We were so lucky to grow up on a farm and learn to feed ourselves and our neighbors. And people don't have the money to see a doctor. Lord, this is the worst time in our history. The Forties have got to be better!

I think it is important for us to know what is going on in the world. The newspapers don't always get the story right. I have read some things that I knew were untrue. Or at least they were slanted toward what one party or another wants you to think. We all have radios now. Tune into President Roosevelt's fireside chats. The radio is his voice and his ideas. It is not reporters distorting the truth. FDR gives us information in a way that we can understand and explains his next idea to turn this country around. I really admire that man.

Well, as usual, I have written more than the Nash Round-Robin Letter rules allow. Dianne would be disappointed. But she could not care less now. She is dancing with Joe, Momma, and Daddy.

And Caroline, thank you for the birthday wishes. It was uneventful birthday.

I love you both to the moon and back,

Annie

August 1941

Annie
Missing My Family

Annie sent a telegram to me asking that I come to Washington. It said that she was sick and could barely take care of herself. "I need my sister," it said. Of course, I went right away. Marie and Suzy came along. They could all stay in Annie's rooming house. I told the girls it would be like a camping trip. They would take the train for the first time. We were all excited and I was anxious about what I might find. Annie tells how love can cure. Not only the love from her sister but also from children and the right man.

I haven't been able to sleep. If I get three hours a night, that is good. My head hurts, I feel like I have a fever. I have missed work or come home early for a week. Once my cough started, they told me not to come back until it goes away.

Jon gave me the address for a doctor. I am sure he is worried about me, but he is probably more afraid he might catch something from me. I am not even sure if I have enough energy to bathe and get to the doctor. Since we have a telephone at work, Jon called Dr. Finch and scheduled an appointment for tomorrow. Jon is sending a car for me in the morning. He said, "No excuses! Get your sweet self to the doc."

I sent a telegram to Ethel. I really need to see family. She and the girls will be here in two days. This ordeal is going on longer than I can ever remember being sick before. The longer I am sick, the more depressed I feel and a little scared.

Liquids, rest, and a shot of whiskey with honey is what Momma would say. But at home that worked in just a few days. I am reading at night, hoping to make myself sleepy. I'm about halfway through Steinbeck's *Grapes of Wrath*. Not a good book choice to stop being sad. But I can't put it down. I love the way he describes a scene and gets me into the characters. Those characters win the pitiful award. Whew, I thought our life on the farm was hard!

I did sleep better last night but still feel exhausted. Today I will see the doctor and get some medicine. Maybe I will be up and around by the time Ethel arrives.

Dr. Finch's office was full of sick people. Five people were in the waiting room when I arrived. All looked like some variation of near death. I wanted to wait outside, but the nurse had me take a seat. She gave me a glass of water and said, "Looks like you could use this. It's okay, it's clean."

Maybe I looked worse than I thought.

It turns out I actually was sicker than I thought. The

doctor did not do much of an exam before telling me he was sending me to the hospital. I objected, "All I need is some medicine. My sister is coming with my nieces, and I need to be home when they arrive."

His matter-of-fact approach made me pay attention. "You do not need to be around your sister. You have advanced stage influenza. We will give you medicine, but most importantly, you need to be with nurses day and night."

The next thing I remember is going to the hospital in an ambulance. I think the sirens were screaming. Or was it just me? I felt a cloth over my face. It was damp with some foul smelling medicine.

After the best sleep I have ever had, I opened my eyes to see Ethel there. She was sitting beside my bed holding my hand. Tears streamed from my eyes. It was so good to see my sister. Ethel told me I had been mostly asleep for three days. She said, "I started to worry about whether you would wake up. I want to meet this Jonathan fella who keeps bringing flowers every day."

She gave me a Nash girl's hug and told me about it. "You sure enough have the flu, little girl. They have been cooling your fever with wet rags, keeping you asleep with medicine, and giving you fresh orange juice with a pill to help with aches and pains. Dr. Finch comes by each morning to check on you. I asked what can be done to make you well. He said, 'There's nothing we can do except what we are doing. A strong body can often take care of this—and faith.' You had me scared! I am glad for you to see me."

I asked her where Marie and Suzy were and she told me she and the girls had taken a taxi cab to my rooming house from the train station. My friends there told her I was in the hospital. They offered to keep the girls so Ethel could come to the hospital to see me. Ethel was going back to the rooming house at night to be with the girls. I had to laugh when Ethel said my friends had cleaned my room of all the cooties before she and the girls arrived! It's a good thing I told them my sister and nieces were coming!

Of course, Ethel wanted to talk about Jon. She said, "Mr. Walsh sneaks by to see you every evening and brings these flowers. The nurses say he is as handsome as Clark Gable. He sits by your bed and talks for an hour or so. Yowza! Annie, it looks like you have landed a really good man."

That made me feel so happy. Ethel and all my friends at the rooming house cared for me. I had no clue Jon would be so attentive, so Ethel's news was exciting. I asked her what time it was.

Ethel looked at her watch and grinned. She said, "He should be here any minute. I won't stick around to meet him tonight. I'll let you two be and go to your place and get it ready for you to come home. But tell him so far I approve of him."

Early the next morning Dr. Finch checked in on me. "Well, well, Annie. You seemed to have kicked the flu hard! I am glad to see you looking so well."

He gave me instructions to stay home and rest. He said since my body was still compromised that I should not go to work or be around crowds. He told me to give it a few more days and to keep taking the aspirin, drink plenty of orange juice, and eat when I was hungry. Oh, and to nap at least an hour every day.

I grabbed his hand and squeezed it and said, "I can do that, Doctor. Thank you. Thank you. I feel so well!"

I had time to bathe and get dressed before Ethel came through the door. I was sitting up in bed diving into a bowlful of buttered grits, just like momma used to make. I greeted her with "I am going home today, Sis! I can't wait to see those girls!"

Ethel admired the giant bouquet of red roses on the night table and asked me to tell her about last night with Prince Charming. I gave her the highlights then smiled like I had a secret and said, "Jon and I both think I must be well. He said I had lots of vitality." Ethel raised her eyebrows and said, "Does he now? It must have been quite the reunion."

A weird silence fell over Ethel, then I remembered how it feels to be sad for the want of something you don't have. I have felt jealous and sad much of the time because I don't have a children like my sisters. I wondered if Ethel felt that way because Jon is here for me but George is gone.

As if she could read my mind Ethel said, "I am so happy for you, baby sister. You have a really good man around. These are the times I really miss George. When he was killed trying to fix that truck that slipped off the jack and fell on him, I thought I would never be happy again. I remembered that ridiculous children's book Dianne told me about—*The Little Engine that Could.* Just like Dianne had to do when she lost Joe, I know I will have to get over losing George, someday somehow. Today is that kind of day—seeing you so happy."

We left the hospital together, bringing the roses with us. Ethel had delivered the other flowers to people in my ward who had no flowers. A blue car drove up and stopped at the front of the hospital just as we were walking out. "That's a fine jalopy!" I shouted to the driver. I was admiring the whitewalls and convertible top. The driver stepped out and asked, "Want a ride, dolls?"

"Heck yeah!" Ethel said.

I ran over and planted a kiss on the driver's luscious lips. Ethel laughed and said, "You better be Jon Walsh!" After a long dreamy kiss, Jon smiled back at Ethel and said, "You are darn right I better be!"

It is not like Ethel to chatter on and on, but she did on the trip home. She talked about the car, Washington, how quickly I got well (according to the doctor), and her daughters. Then she became more like Ethel and said, "Mr. Walsh, you seem like a good guy with a good job, but I have to tell you Annie is really the only sister I have close now, and if you hurt her, I am going to come after you!" Jon and I laughed, but I knew she was dead serious. I loved her for that.

Jon dropped us off at the front door of the boarding house. He told us he would let us settle in but would be back at six o'clock with Chinese food for dinner. As I closed the door to the house, Ethel said, "Chinese food? What the heck?"

"You are gonna love it!" I said. "So will the girls. You eat it with chopsticks." Ethel just shook her head.

Suzy and Marie were on the couch in the parlor. They ran to me, then stopped a foot away. "Can we hug you, Aunt Annie?" Marie asked, and from Suzy came, "Are you all well now?"

"You are darn tootin' I'm better, and you must give me hugs! Lots of them!"

They ran in for hugs, and I realized how tall the girls were getting. Of course, the tears came, and I looked at Ethel and said, "Nash girls hug, right here! Come on in, Ethel!"

All four of us sat on the couch and talked about their trip up to Washington on the train, what it was like to sleep in a hospital, all the ladies that live in this house, and everything else the young ones could think of.

Marie changed the subject. "Mom says you have a boyfriend. Can we meet him? He is nice?"

"He is nice, Marie. He may be the nicest man I have ever met. He has an important job in the government. He can be very serious, but also gentle." Ethel cleared her throat to signal that was enough talk about gentleness.

"He is bringing us dinner tonight, so you will get to meet him. He's dreamy!"

Ethel decided after we all got to know him we would think up a song about him. Suzy was most excited about that. "I love the songs you make up, Mom!" I looked at Ethel with loving envy at Suzy now able to call Ethel *mom*.

Jon arrived with a large bag full of folded paper cartons. As he unpacked all the food, I brought plates and bowls for the Chow Mein, rice, and egg rolls. I suggested he leave the fortune cookies for dessert. Marie and Suzy could not figure out how to use the chopsticks. They watched closely as Jon pulled the noodles into his mouth and tried to copy his technique. After several attempts, I handed the girls forks. They dove into the rice and Chow Mein. After more success with her fork, Marie said, "This is nearly as good as your chicken and dumplings, Mom."

During dinner there were a million questions for Jon not only from the girls but also Ethel. He held up well during the inquisition. After all, he's a military man.

Jon stood from the table and said, "I am sorry to say this, ladies, but I must retire for the evening. I have a full day tomorrow. Before bedtime, open the fortune cookies and see if they have any news about your future."

Jon leaned over to me and said quietly, "There are two more work days this week, and I need to be there." To the whole group he said, "On Saturday I'll come back and take you all sightseeing in Washington." Everyone was excited about that. I felt like I knew every inch of D.C. now, but I wanted to see it from Jon's eyes and in that gorgeous car!

Ethel announced bedtime for everyone because we all needed good sleep. Suzy reminded her that there were cookies to eat. I showed them how to crack open the cookie and find the strip of paper inside.

I had to laugh when Marie said, "That is one strange looking cookie. Can we eat it?"

I told them of course they could but read their fortune first.

Marie said, "Mine doesn't make sense. *Those that live in a glass house should not throw stones.*"

Ethel said, "It means don't be mean or others will pound you!" We all giggled.

Suzy said, "Mine makes sense! It says *Sing every day and chase the mean blues away.* We do that most days!"

Marie wanted to know what Ethel's fortune said. My no-nonsense sister said, "Mine makes no sense at all. These are not really fortunes, just sayings to sell a cookie. Anyway, it says *Expect the Unexpected.* Well,

I definitely have learned how to do that!"

I waited until the others were finished, then I read mine aloud. *You will be happy with your spouse.* That got smiles from everyone. Well, if I had one, I certainly would be.

Ethel reminded us what was next with a firm, "Okay, girls, off to bed while Annie figures out how to land a husband!"

The girls went to the bedroom to lay out their sheet, blanket, and pillows on the floor next to my bed. I was getting tired so joined them in the room to change into my pajamas. I told the girls I wanted to read them a book I bought just for them. They hopped up on the bed and snuggled up to me. Ethel went to the parlor to clean up dinner dishes. The story I read them was *Make Way for Ducklings.* It's about some mallard ducks that decide to raise their family in a big city pond. I must have fallen asleep as quickly as the girls.

In the morning I opened my eyes to the sunlight peeking through the curtains. I could hear the rhythmic breathing of two sweet girls next to me. There was a strong sense that Momma was watching and smiling.

"Good morning, sunshine!" I said as I entered the kitchen where Ethel was cooking eggs in Momma's cast iron pan. The smell of bacon was what lured me out of bed. And yes, buttered grits were simmering in the pot on the stove.

Ethel smiled at me and said, "Morning, sleepyhead. We have a lot to talk about before the girls are up. Have a seat. Breakfast is nearly ready. I want to hear about your intentions with Jon. He seems like a great guy. Is there anything crazy in his background?"

I said, "Nope, nothing that I know about. He is a good man and a great dad."

Ethel jumped right on that last part. "WHAT? He has children?"

I told her the whole story as I knew it. Jon had been married. His wife died in childbirth. His daughter, Lisa, is just turning one. He has a fulltime housekeeper who takes care of Lisa while he works. Jon's job is important, and he is dedicated to it.

I told her how devoted he is to his daughter and to his work. I used to think there was no room for me, but the last few weeks have shown me he wants to add me to his life. He told me before he left last night that meeting Ethel and the girls sealed the deal for him. He wants to move this relationship forward. When I told Ethel that part, she came over to me, swallowing me in her arms and said, "Oh, my sweet sister. I am beyond happy for you. But take it slow. I don't want this to be like all the others. Make sure he is right for you. Not just you being right for him."

You just have to love a sister like that!

June 1945

Ethel
Decisions, Decisions

Life is about daily choices. The Nash sisters know that with a plan choices are easier to make. All three of us remaining sisters have our own individual plans. With telephones readily available now, we have frequent conversations to help each stay on track. Marie was ready for college. I wanted her to be the first Nash woman with a college degree. Caroline was more stable and independent in life. And Annie was good. With Larry's help, I started my own ice cream shop in Haw River, just outside of Burlington. To make it through the slow winter months, we also did laundry for the locals. I told people my business tag line was, "I serve you sweets and wash your drawers!"

"What is it about the men in our lives?" I asked Annie on the phone. "Frank couldn't be bothered with us, Larry left, and George got himself killed at work. He and Joe were good men. Joe worked himself to death for Burlington Mills. And your Jon . . . since we all celebrated V Day in May, when will he come home?"

Annie said, "Let's not be so depressing. It is hard to not worry. I don't know when Jon will be coming home, but I think it could be anytime now. Lisa, Jon Jr., and I will throw a big party when he does!" And then she brought up Larry, neatly changing the subject, which she is so good at. "But Ethel, Larry's back and very good to you." Then she asked how the ice cream business was going.

That distracted me and I told her about my little episode with the city government. They raised the tax on business and didn't tell me. I got a citation for unpaid taxes. The city police came and took me to jail. They charged me with something, took my mug shot, and told me to pay my taxes. I told them I would not pay the increase because I had not been adequately notified. So, they put me in a cell and said I would stay there until I paid up. How dare they take advantage of a widow! I could have died in there. Okay, well, maybe not died but anyway. . .

I imagined Annie shaking her head on the other end of the telephone. She hollered, "Oh SUGAR! How did you get out?"

I told her some anonymous person paid my taxes the next morning. The newspaper came and took my picture and did a story about "Woman jailed over $5.00." That was embarrassing for the town and the county, so they let me out. I think it was Larry who paid the taxes. It was more than $5.00, by the way.

Annie was clearly exasperated. She huffed at me. "Good God, Ethel. This is embarrassing for all of us.

Some newsman could pick up the story and examine our whole family. What were you thinking?"

I said I was thinking I didn't have the tax money, and they should have given me warning! And I was thinking they won't do that to me again. I wash the underwear of most people in town, and they like me keeping my mouth shut. Many of my neighbors came by to tell me they would pay my taxes next year.

The telephone is a good way to talk to people. I can hear when I get people riled up. Annie was fit to be tied, so I moved on.

"I want Marie to go to college. The closest one is in Raleigh—State College. We are going to drive up there next week to look around. We'll go visit Caroline while we are there. The Pollard bank account will cover Marie's tuition for all four years. I am excited to see her make something of herself. She is not crazy about the idea. She says I need her here. I do like having her around, but Suzy, Larry, and I can manage things. Suzy has her mind on going to school right here in the county when it is her time."

Annie paused a moment to calm down before she started talking. Then she started preaching to me. She said, "Ethel, Marie going to college fits right in your plan for life. I am glad you are doing that for her. But going to jail fits no plan. In fact, it wrecks it. This business fits in your plan. You are a woman of means, not a lowlife. Act like one, please! You have plenty of money to pay taxes!"

But she wasn't finished after that tirade. She had more to say. "And another thing, Larry is also a good man who made a mistake years ago. You pushed away

Frank. Don't do the same with Larry. He's been back for years now and you just keep him dangling. Go tell him thank you for helping you out. He needs to know he is appreciated. Why don't you marry that man?"

"We will get married in a church someday," I told. "That is in the plan. We almost got married before, but that didn't make him stay around. If at some point Larry and I have a real wedding, he might just stay around because he is supposed to. Now he stays around because he wants to."

"Ethel, that is ridiculous! You once told me to find a man that is good enough for me, not one that I'm good enough for. Larry is that man for you! Doggonit, Ethel, marry that man before he gets tired of waiting!" Then she hung up the phone. You just gotta love a sister like that!

I had the table set. Soup and sandwiches were waiting. When Larry came in, I said, "Larry, I don't think I ever thanked you for springing me from the slammer. Thank you. And thank you for all that you do for me and the girls."

Larry looked straight at my face then looked my whole body up and down for something. He grabbed both of my arms and said, "What the heck, Ethel? Are you sick? Did you see Jesus or something?"

I burst out laughing, "No, Larry. I am fine. Just found a crack in that mean side of me."

He raised my right arm over his head and spun me around. "Well, let me get a better look at that crack!"

We both sat at the table and ate lunch together. Usually he eats while I buzz around the kitchen. He said, "I like this, but I didn't bust you from jail. You were being too stubborn for me to want to help. But I did hate seeing you in that jail." Then he said that I didn't look good behind bars. Good to know.

It was quiet until we heard the horn of a car. "Shoot, can't they even wait for me to have lunch?" I said more to myself than to Larry.

I started to get up to see who was there. Larry held me back and said, "Where is that crack of sweetness, Ethel? Let's keep it here for a while. It's probably somebody picking up their laundry. Remember you have that sign out there that says 'Honk for service.' I'll go."

He went out the door. I heard Larry say, "How can I help you?"

I heard a familiar voice answer, "Is E, I mean is Ethel here?" I stiffened.

"She is. Come on in," responded Larry.

As a man approached the screen door, I knew who it was right away. There were those blue eyes and perfect teeth. I summoned my sweetness and pushed back the anger that rises, even seventeen years later, at the sound of his voice.

Frank said, "Hey, Ethel, you look good!" He looked around for a moment and then he said, "I came to ask you something. And I want to talk to Marie, if I may."

I couldn't think of what to say, especially trying to use my nice tone. Larry spoke up to give me time to think what to say.

"Good to see you, Frank. Come in and have a cup of coffee. I need to go back to the washing machines."

Larry looked toward me and his silent smile said, *Come on, girl. You can do this.*

I moved toward Frank and offered him a chair. "Marie is not here. She spends most of the summer days with her friends doing what teenagers do. I have something to tell you." I was going to tell him about State College. Then I said, "But you go first."

I could tell Larry had not gone far. He was probably standing in the hall so he could listen in.

"Thank you, Ethel. I won't try to explain all that I have done wrong again. I have told you a thousand times. There is no excuse."

I said, "Good, Frank. 'Cause I am tired of hearing it. You have tried to make amends. Sometimes that is all we can do." I was surprised my words came out so nice. But it was true. We can't keep hashing out the past. Then I asked him why he came.

Those blue eyes gazed straight into mine, almost melting the rest of the anger I have for him. "I have found a woman that I would like to marry. I am here to ask permission from you and Marie."

The lump in my throat felt the size of a peach pit. I looked away for a moment trying to find Larry. I cleared my throat, "Well, Frank, I knew this would happen at some time. I imagined it already had. You do not need my permission. But I like the fact that you wanted to tell Marie before you got married. Marie never asked questions about you, Frank. Even after I told her the truth in 1941, she didn't want to know more than I told her. She understood you were my first beau and her biological daddy. But other than that she was not curious. She knows you have set aside money for her. I think she would like to know that you are getting married and will have a family. Marie should be back around dinner time. Maybe you can come back and see her then."

"Ethel, I would appreciate that. Her name is Elizabeth. She works with me at the law office."

I cut him off. "I don't need to know about her."

"Okay," he said lowering his eyes to the floor. He paused then asked, "What was it you wanted to tell me?"

I stepped toward the door to the hall and called out, "Larry, come in here, you sly dog. I know you are hiding."

Larry came into the room looking like a kid caught with his hand in the cookie jar. "Frank, I wanted to tell you that Larry and I are going to get married."

Larry looked at me and his mouth dropped open. He took one step at a time toward me like someone playing *Mother May I*. Putting his arm around my waist he said, "We are? Oh, I mean, yes, Frank, we are! Heck, I've been asking her to marry me in the eyes of God for years. Finally, we are going to do it. Yaaahoo!"

Frank laughed. Probably because he knew exactly what Larry was going through. You never can tell when I am going to be ready. You just have to wait. There were handshakes all around. I hadn't touched Frank since 1928, and it was weirdly familiar. I shifted to put my arms around Larry in a big hug, threw my head back, and with great relief, shouted, "It is a happy day!"

After Marie came back from dinner with Frank, her face was blotched. She had a soggy man's handkerchief wadded up in her hand. She said, "Mom, he's getting married. He is marrying a woman he works with. He told me all about her. He said I would really like her. I won't like her. I don't have to like her. This is his life not mine. Why does he think I care?"

I pulled her to me, and I talked with her head on my chest. "Honey, you are his daughter. Even though I pushed him away from us, he really cares about you. I am not surprised he is getting married, but I am shocked he came to ask permission. That counts for something. At one point in our lives, he and I loved each other. I don't think that ever goes away. That love just changes into caring. Let him care for you. The best thing about Frank and Ethel is you."

Later that evening, Caroline called. She is allowed access to the phone twice a week. Monday is usually the day she calls Annie. I get a call from her on Friday night.

"Hey, big sister!" she said in a cheery voice. "I can't tell wait to tell you about my day."

"Okay, shoot," I replied.

"Dr. Redmond called me into his office. Nurse Joanna, one of my favorite nurses, was there. Belle was too. Doc said after the battery of tests they had done on me and my bodily functions, they wanted to report I am much better. It is stupid they need tests to show that. I could have told them I was. But anyway, they reduced some of my meds a few months ago, and I have not needed a shock treatment in a long time. Belle came over and sat next to me. Maybe she thought I would have a fit or something. I just sat there trying to process the information. Then Belle said, "Caroline, you are moving out of Dix Hill. There is a family that needs someone to do light housekeeping and care for their two children. They travel a lot and want someone reliable. They are hoping you will come live with them."

"Wait! Wait a darn minute!" I shouted over the phone. "I don't know anything about you moving out. They have not talked to me. Are you telling the truth?"

"The doctor said you and Annie were sent a letter with a summary of the report. The letter also explained the plan for my next treatment, which is living off campus. When I talked to Annie, she said she got the letter and was so happy for me."

Out of fear I began shooting questions like arrows. "I didn't get a letter. I just talked to Annie today and she didn't mention anything. I am worried about this. How do we know these are good people? Where will you live? How old are these children? Will they pay you or is this unpaid work? What about your criminal record?"

Caroline said, "Stop, Ethel!" Her voice was stern but there was no anger or agitation in her voice. I got quiet. She said, "I can tell you all the details. Annie just wanted me to have a chance to tell you myself! Just let me talk!"

I was not sure how to process all this. Caroline said, "I am almost 30 years old now. According to the law, I am no longer a ward of the court. I am considered able to make decisions. The doctors and nurses all met to discuss me, as they usually do, but this time it was about how well I am doing. This family lives in Raleigh in a place called Oakwood. It is a big house. I would have my own room and kitchen. I know they are good people because it is Belle's son and daughter-in-law. I have met them many times but never knew this was in the works. Belle's son is an architect and a professor at State College. He travels all over the United States teaching building design. The children are two and four. The mother is very nice. She invited me to stay overnight at their house this weekend to get to know them. They are letting me make this decision."

I was totally flabbergasted. This was my youngest sister, my sometimes crazy sister, my former criminal sister, and she sounded like an adult. A really smart adult. Someone who was really thinking carefully to make the right decision.

"And, Ethel," she added, "they are going to pay me really well. I can begin to pay you and Annie back for all the things you have done for me. When you come next week with Marie and Suzy, I want you to meet them."

I realized I had not said a word through all this. It was because I was bursting with emotion. I was stunned and happy and so very proud. I said, "Oh, Caroline, this sounds wonderful. Belle knows you better than we do. She is the perfect person to watch over you. And I know she has a family that is just as perfect. What could be better?"

My tears were spilling onto the phone receiver. "I can't wait to meet them. And I am so proud of you, my smart and most capable sister."

I could tell she was crying too. Not the sad tears we all usually shed but the happiest ones.

I used words our mother said so often. Now I believed them—truly.

"The Nash girls are doing just fine. Praise God."

NOTES . . .

THE NASH SISTERS FREQUENTLY SANG to celebrate, get through hard times, or find their courage. They often created their own words to the tunes of familiar songs.

- The Doxology in Chapter 2 was written for song in 1674 by Thomas Ken.

- From chapter 4, "Jesus Loves Me" was written as a poem by Anna Bartlett Warner in 1859 and put to music in 1862 by William Batchelder Bradbury. The sisters put their own words to the tune.

- The sisters all remembered their momma singing "Rock a bye, Baby." In chapter 6 Ethel sings it to Marie. This poem turned lullaby was published in 1765 as a poem and in 1805 found its way into Benjamin Tabart's *Songs for the Nursery*.

- In chapter 7, Diane calms down a situation with her rendition of "America the Beautiful," which was written by Katharine Lee Bates as a poem and published in 1893 and in 1910 Samuel Bates put it to music.

- "Skiddy-Mer-Rink-A-Doo Means I Love You" was written by Felix Feist with music by Al Piantadosi and published in 1910. The Nash sisters had a sisterly moment singing this nonsensical word song, adding their own flair to it in chapter 8.

ACKNOWLEDGMENTS

My husband has been my rock and motivator. He is the one who got me to "finally write that book." Without him I would not have had the guts to do it. Thank you, honey.

My grandnieces were the first people to see Marie's account in this book. They helped me get the voices of the children right. Thank you, Perry, Peyton, Maddie, and Avery.

And talk about courage! During editing, my editor helped me find the courage like the Cowardly Lion, the brain like the Scarecrow, and the heart to keep my heart in the words like the Tin Man. Thank you, Lee Heinrich.

And finally thank you, Noyes Capehart Long, for caring for my sister and allowing me to benefit from your talent on the cover of this book.

A Message from the Author

Dear Readers,

It has been great fun to write about life and the events that shape us into who we are, especially when things go off the rails a bit. I admit to having plenty of life experience to draw from. I hope you enjoyed the characters and what they had to say in *The Nash Sisters*. Please come back for more stories of the Nash women and the men they allow in their lives in upcoming books!

In the meantime, would you please leave a review of *The Nash Sisters* on *Amazon.com* or Goodreads or anywhere else you found this book. The reviews are so important for helping a book get found by other readers. As any author will tell you, reviews just add wind to our sails!

Gratefully yours and until next time . . .
Leatha Marie

Made in the USA
Middletown, DE
17 November 2019

78929829R00094